Sweet Inspirations

LOVE HAPPENS • BOOK NINE

SUSAN WARNER

Sweet Inspirations

One

"You! Thief, stop!"

Elizabeth Butler ran down the empty sidewalk. She was very aware there was barely anyone on the street. While both sides of the street were populated with houses, it was as if everyone had all gone out at the same time. This town was such a huge contrast to living in New York. Had she been in New York now, several people would have stopped if for no other reason than to glare at the sheer nosiness.

The thief looked up and seemed confused. Elizabeth hoped he didn't think that the afternoon sun highlighting his sable brown hair and his easy-going smile were going to distract her from the facts. He was stealing her precious.

She had just made the sprint in her two-inch black pumps—which were very comfortable for walking in but obviously not made for running—when she thought, *If I had known I might have to run, I would have switched into sneakers like every other city girl does when she's not at work.* She should have known some things wouldn't change. In the city or in the country a woman had to be prepared for anything.

"You there, I can't believe you'd try to steal in broad daylight!"

The thief still looked confused. Elizabeth didn't let that stop her. She reached out and grabbed her precious package from his hands. Then she took a step back and surreptitiously looked up and down the block for someone who she could call for help if need be.

"Listen, lady, I'm no thief."

Elizabeth turned back and gave him a hard stare. "Okay, Mr. I'm so hot I can do what I want, if you're no thief, what were you doing with my Smiley?"

"Smiley?"

"Yes, Smiley, the small bundle of joy you were about to abscond with!"

"Oh, the dog!"

Elizabeth covered Smiley's long floppy brown ears.

"Would you show a little sensitivity?" she hissed at the thief.

He actually looked confused. "I think he knows he's a dog. I'm thinking that tail and four legs thing gave him a clue," the thief said with a smile.

Tapping her right foot, she held Smiley closer to herself. She looked down at Smiley, and he looked back at her with large, brown eyes and gave her a quick lick on the chin. He wasn't as spry as he had once been, but he was still as faithful as ever. Thinking about the drama he must have gone through, she turned on the thief.

"Listen, I don't know what your thing is, but stealing a dog is the lowest of low."

"Okay, this has gone on long enough. I didn't steal your dog; he was walking out here by himself, and I picked him up."

Elizabeth stopped and looked up the block to see she had indeed left the car door open while she was going in and out of the flower shop. She was having some plants delivered, and she was told the florist was the best person to talk to about holding plants. Elizabeth had to admit it sounded weird to her that the florist would also offer the service to hold on to her plants, but it was a small town in Florida called Sweet Blooms, she should have expected they do things a little differently.

She supposed if Smiley had been bored, he would have come. Smiley usually ran from noises and was very jittery. Since she'd come to Sweet Blooms a week ago, she had seen a whole change in his behavior. Smiley's nervousness was down, and his barking was to a minimum. She knew she had made the right decision to move to Sweet Blooms and open up her dog sanctuary. Well, she was sure until the thief.

"I bet you did pick him up."

"Listen, he's an older dog, and he seemed really sweet, so I picked him up. Not so I could steal him, but so I could take him somewhere besides the street to live."

"Ah-ha. So you were taking Smiley, my dog, and you were going to give him away to another person."

The thief opened his mouth and then closed it. "Listen, why don't we start this over? My name is Henry Jenkins," he said as he extended his hand out.

Elizabeth wanted to groan out loud. He wasn't some good-looking thief in a small town, she thought to herself. Henry Jenkins was the reason she was in Sweet Blooms. Although he wasn't what she thought he would be. She thought he would be about seventy years old and wearing overalls.

Instead, Henry Jenkins was a very attractive man by anyone's standards. He wasn't the perfect ideal, but he had warm brown eyes that went along with his brushed-back hair. His nose was a little crooked and he had a dimple on each cheek and one on his chin. He had a beard that was reddish-brown and beckoned her to touch it to see if it was as soft as it looked. What made the beard even more noticeable was the way he had shaped it. The beard was low on his cheeks and light on the chin.

Henry Jenkins was not the elderly gentleman she thought she was coming to see. No, Henry Jenkins was just the kind of man Elizabeth was trying to avoid. God made men look this good to hide their two-timing, opportunistic natures. If everyone saw them clearly, they'd never make it to adulthood.

Elizabeth knew this was her old baggage rearing its ugly head. All men were not like her ex, Lance Classon. Lance had the features of the best sculpture and the heart of the darkest villain. Maybe Henry was different. Maybe he wasn't selfish, self-absorbed, and shallow.

"I can tell from your speechlessness that you've rethought this situation and realize that I'm the Good Samaritan here. I mean, however it happened, the dog got free and I saved him," Henry said with a large smile on his face that only deepened his dimples. Those dimples were like a bucket of cold water being tossed on Elizabeth.

"This is so not going to work," she muttered.

"What?"

Elizabeth didn't even answer. Instead, she turned away from Henry and started walking back towards her car.

"Hey, what's not going to work, and what's your name? The hero usually gets something from the people he rescues."

Elizabeth stopped and pivoted on her heel. When she turned, she turned into a wall of muscle that wrapped itself around her and Smiley. For a moment, the world was blocked out and she was engulfed in a cloud of soap, strength, and man. The feeling was foreign but welcome. For a few moments, she forgot he was a thief, and the woman in her took a sigh of relief. That feeling lasted all of a moment. Then she was being let go, and the only thing she heard was the profuse sputtering of Henry.

"So, so sorry. I didn't expect you to turn around so quickly."

Elizabeth steadied herself and then stood with her hands on her hips. "Okay, we need to get some things cleared up Superman. We're in a small town, so I'm going to give you a pass for not being able to tell the difference between a lost dog and one that wandered off course a bit."

"Ouch! You're a tough lady."

"Please, let's not recap. More importantly, I need to ask you, what were you doing here by the florist?" Elizabeth asked.

He grinned at her and folded his arms over his chest. What was it about him, anyway? Every move he made was like he was posing for one of those sexy commercials where no one really knows what is being sold. Really, she knew better. Gorgeous men were about as trustworthy as a two-dollar bill.

"As it turns out, I was looking for you."

The statement caught Elizabeth off guard and had her falling back to her original thought. Gorgeous men couldn't be trusted.

"You don't even know my name," she incredulously.

"Well, I don't really need to know your name to know you're the one I'm looking for."

"Oh for Pete's sake, is this some lame pick-up line?"

Henry laughed and shook his head. "You are definitely new. Let me explain. You see, an unmarried woman arrived in town today. I know you're not married because you stopped at the garage—Old lady Winston was there. She happened to notice you didn't have a ring and that your ring finger was all one color. She took that to mean you weren't married or had been divorced for a while."

Elizabeth could feel the shock spreading across her face. "Are you talking about that sweet lady who asked me to walk her to her car?"

Henry nodded. "The same. While you were helping her, she was evaluating your hands. When you left the garage, you stopped at Sweet Blooms Cafe. Before you even arrived at Sweet Blooms, Mrs. Winston had called Rose, one of the owners of Sweet Blooms Café, to let her know there was a nice, eligible woman in town. Rose noticed you when you picked up a bagel but you were constantly looking out towards your car. So when you left the cafe, she called Agnes to find out if she was going to bridge, and to let her know there was a nice woman who had either a pet or a child—from your looking back at your car of course—who was single and was planning to come to the courthouse. When you arrived at the courthouse, you spoke to Clarissa. After talking to you, Clarissa called me and said there was a new, single woman come to town. Clarissa said you were asking about me but went to the floral shop. The way gossip was running Clarissa thought I needed to save you before the rest of them started adding to the telephone game."

Elizabeth had heard the rumors about towns and gossip, but this was a bit much. "Not that it matters, but I don't have kids and I was never married," she echoed in a daze.

"I could tell," he said.

And there it went. All of the goodwill Elizabeth thought she was going to have towards him went up in smoke.

"Don't finish that thought. No good can come from it. In fact, maybe you should stop while you're ahead and we can meet some other time."

Instead of taking the hint she so kindly offered him, his smile widened before he said, "You've got grit, as my mama would have said."

"I've had to get some, I wasn't born with it. Which means I know when to use it and when not to."

"You know, I've got that knack. I bring out the best in people."

"You are one step from me—" Elizabeth let out a deep breath.

"Listen, we don't have to talk about me. I totally get it, and I'm glad I could be here for you."

She turned around to take Smiley back to the car. His head was lolling and there was something suspiciously warm on her arm that she didn't want to look too closely at until she was in the car. She needed to have some space between her and tall, dark, and arrogant.

She was a woman with some issues and a mission. This man aggravated both her issues and her mission. He set off all of her internal alarms that said she should run quickly and stuff cotton in her ears. He was the equivalent of a male siren. Elizabeth had decided to go the road of least resistance if she should ever decide to get into another relationship. Yes, she'd want a quiet man who was unassuming and just happy to be with someone.

Second, if for some reason she threw caution to the wind and decided he'd be a good option for a small-town love, she'd have to work too hard for him to notice her. Men like him wanted women who could cook, clean, and iron.

She had visited Sweet Blooms four times now, and she'd visited every take out restaurant and diner. Cooking wasn't on her list of skills. In fact, she anticipated she'd be losing some weight because it appeared the town of Sweet Blooms closed by ten, which by her standards was the end of dinner and the beginning of snack time. She wouldn't even go into how she knew every cleaning service, drop off laundry and dry cleaners.

Every time Elizabeth had been in a relationship, she had lost to career and money. What she had learned from those failed relationships was who she really was.

She was resilient. She had survived losing it all from living in posh condos to living in a shelter.

She was loving. When she was at her lowest, Smiley had come to her as a fellow stray, and she had shared her food with him.

But most of all, she was focused. When she had made up her mind to get herself and Smiley off of the streets, nothing had stopped her. She didn't need to be the perfect company to Henry Jenkins. She didn't need a Henry Jenkins in her life at all, she just needed Henry Jenkins' land.

"So, Elizabeth, did you want to talk later?"

"What?" she quipped, frustrated to be caught so deep in her own thoughts and irritated that he stopped her right before she was in her car. She adored Smiley, but he could stand to lose a few pounds.

Henry waved his hand between them. "I'm only asking because you're moving away from me at top speed. I could keep following you, but what will the town think then?"

She inhaled a deep breath. He was right. Unfortunately, she wasn't in the right space to even utter those words to him right now. "How about we try for later today?"

"We're actually scheduled to meet in the morning." He gave her a grin that she just knew he must have practiced. It was the kind of slow-motion grin that happened in three seconds, but when she saw it, it occurred in slow motion. In her mind, she imagined his chest puffing out a little farther. He turned his head to the left because that was his best side. Then when he smiled, he gave her the best view of the perfectly proportioned lips and that dimple that said, "Come on, you know you want to fall for me."

"So, Elizabeth, I'll see you at my place in the morning?"

Later she thought. That's right, she was going to go to his place, later on, to see if his land was the new home for her business. If it was, she would be seeing Mr. Walking Temptation every day. "Of course I'll be there."

He tipped his head and walked away. Elizabeth looked at him as he sauntered down the block.

She wondered if anyone was peering out of the houses as he went. She shook her head and continued with Smiley to the car.

Dogs she understood, she thought. If you stayed with them and treated them fairly, then they'd stay with you forever. The male species, however, was a largely unknown enigma. Henry's type was the worst. He smiled and appeared like he was interested, but she would just never know.

I mean, she knew better than to build a lifetime commitment based on a smile. She wasn't that young or innocent anymore. Elizabeth had been burned enough to know that taking men on face value was the path to getting hurt. All that being said, Henry Jenkins was still a fine-looking man. For an instant when he smiled, she had a butterfly or two flutters in her stomach.

The good news was her ex hadn't soured her ability to appreciate a man. The bad news was the man who seemed to have caught her eye was the man she needed to do business with. No matter how good he looked, Elizabeth was going to keep business and pleasure separate from one another.

It wasn't every day that a man had to present a business proposal to his ex and her new husband. That was exactly the position he was in now. He'd sent the research to Adam Cade and his own ex-wife, Hannah. This was a long shot, but he was used to selling long shots. But if this didn't fly, he didn't have a plan B.

He had been shown into Adam Cade's trailer office. The trailer sat on the Cade ranch property. Adam Cade was the owner of the multi-million dollar wood carving business. He was also a native of sweet Blooms. When Adam moved to Sweet Blooms and opened up a business, it had helped Sweet Blooms get on the map. It also meant that if you wanted something done in Sweet Blooms, the quickest way to make sure the council would approve it was to make sure Adam Cade was onboard. Besides having money, Adam was a fair man who believed in giving people second chances. In fact, today Henry was counting on that particular part of his nature.

Henry was sitting in a comfortable high back leather chair on the other side of an even larger desk. The trailer was air-conditioned and the whole effect made him think he had stepped back into a corporate CEO's office. The secretary was missing, but he had been shown to the trailer by one of the farmhands, which would have to be the Sweet Blooms equivalent.

Henry looked at the desk and saw pictures of Hannah smiling in a wedding dress. He saw his son Nathan in the wedding party, and he was happy and sad at the same time. Hannah deserved everything Adam could give her. She was a treasure he hadn't been ready to receive when they were married.

When he looked at Nathan, he was so proud of his son. Despite all of the drama that occurred between Hannah and him, Nathan had turned out to be a well-adjusted young man who knew himself sometimes better than his parents knew themselves.

He let out a breath and tried to review the points in his head. When it was all said and done, he had to make this work. He had money of his own from investments, but they didn't come close to helping him pay off the acres of land he had inherited. He had given the land to Hannah, but she had now moved out of it and to the Cade's land. So he was now sitting on his ancestral land, but he didn't own it. He needed to get the deed back, and then he needed to find a way to make money to support him on the land. He thought he might have found an answer with Elizabeth. He just needed to sell the idea to Hannah and her husband.

Henry didn't have a lot of good memories of this place. Everyone in town knew the Jenkins men had a drinking problem. As soon as he could, he'd left home to find a better place. He had an older brother, but he had left before him. The only memories Henry had of him were of him using his body to shield him from a drunken father. When Henry turned 10, his brother, Konstantine, left home. By the time Henry was sixteen he had worked on the farm long enough to know that he didn't want to be a farmer.

He hadn't set foot back on the land until his father had passed away, and he had brought his then wife, Hannah, to Sweet Blooms. Again the weight and the memories of "Jenkins men" haunted him in the town until it broke his marriage apart.

Now time had passed. Hannah was in love again, and he was happy that she had found a way to move on, even if it wasn't with him. Now, after mending his relationship with his son, Nathan, and becoming friends with Hannah, it was time to clean up his life here in Sweet Blooms. That meant he had to ask Hannah to give him back the deed to his land and then sell her husband, Adam Cade, on what he wanted to do on the land.

Henry had looked high and low for a business that he could run. He was a salesman, and there weren't a lot of opportunities for a salesman. Besides, in the town of Sweet Blooms bargaining was almost impossible unless you were over the age of 60. It appeared that no matter what price you thought you could sell an item, an older person would remind you that they had seen you in your diapers and then tell you the price you'd be selling at.

Then Elizabeth Butler's name came up during one of the council meetings. The idea was new and fit in with the community of Sweet Blooms. This business wouldn't make him rich. It wasn't that kind of business. This was a business where the land would be used, and he'd be able to give something back to someone else.

Just as he was rethinking this plan again, Adam and Hannah walked in. The desk was large, and there were two seats behind it. He stood up and waited for Hannah to sit.

"Please, Henry take a seat," Hannah said as she pulled up a chair next to Adam. Henry thought they made a handsome couple. Hannah's dark hair was pulled into a ponytail, and she had the glow that women get when they're happy. As he watched them sit behind the desk, all of his fears came back. Maybe they wouldn't really like the idea. Maybe Hannah would decide they both would own the land. He gave himself a mental shake and let out a breath, he'd close this sale.

"So Henry, you asked to see the both of us, what can we do for you?" Adam asked.

"Did you get the files I sent over?" Henry asked.

Hannah smiled and nodded at him. Before she could speak, Adam put his hand on her lap and then looked at him.

"We both got the file, but I think I want to hear you explain what it is that you're looking for," Adam said.

Henry nodded. He'd expected this. He was hoping that he didn't have to present in front of them both, but he'd come prepared to give his pitch.

"As you both know, I'm living on the Jenkins land. I'd like two things: I'd like to buy back the Jenkins land that Hannah has in trust to her. I'll of course need a mortgage to do that. The second thing is I'd like to use the land to help a new venture that I've been apprised of. After looking in Sweet Blooms, we seem to have all of the stores we need, with others on the way. I would like to turn the land into a no-kill, senior animal shelter. The land is large enough, and we would combine with the nearby animal shelter. I've been approached by a person who has the same vision I do, and they also have several grants to pay for the room, board, and renovation. The grants are for three years, so it gives me enough time to see if this will work."

He waited for someone to speak. Hannah had been nodding her head all through his speech. He could see the excitement in her eyes. Adam, on the other, hadn't changed expressions. Henry might have thought he hadn't heard a word he said if it weren't for the fact he could see Adam's hand was patting Hannah's offering comfort. He saw it and wondered if he had ever done anything like that for Hannah. Looking up, he saw her smile of happiness and eagerness as he talked about the plan. Henry hoped he was as resilient as Hannah. When he looked at Adam, he saw no sign of how the meeting was going either way.

"So, you want Hannah to give you the land from your divorce so you can rescue senior dogs in the last days of life?"

Henry looked at them both. "Yup, that's about it."

"Why does she have to give up her share?" Adam asked. Henry glanced at Hannah and could see she was a bit distressed.

"It's the term of the grant. They only want to deal with one owner," Henry replied.

"So what do you think about giving Hannah the land and letting her sign and you run it?" Adam asked.

Henry didn't speak. He knew this could have been an option. If he were in Adam's spot, he would ask the same thing. He thought it might come to this, but he had hoped otherwise.

Henry looked at Hannah and gave a small smile, then he turned to Adam.

"It's not my first choice, but yes, I'd agree to that."

Adam smiled and leaned forward. "Fortunately, it won't come to that, but it's good to know where you stand."

Henry felt the relief hit him like a ton of bricks. Happy and confused, he looked at them both.

Hannah finally spoke. "Adam and I had already agreed this was a good idea. He just wanted to make sure your motives were clear."

Henry smiled and nodded, and Hannah and Adam went on and on about how they thought it was a great idea. Henry, on the other hand, was still trying to get his breath. In the space of minutes, he had faced starting over, to losing everything, to getting hope again. If Hannah could give him this chance, he'd make the best of it and be more than anyone ever thought he could. He'd show the town of Sweet Blooms that there was such a thing as a good Jenkins man.

Two

Elizabeth sat in her green Geo Metro and took a deep breath. The car was small, with no air conditioner and had three cylinders under the hood. The man who sold her the car told her the engine would never be fast, but it was reliable and would get her where she needed to be. Today she found herself in front of a two-story house that looked like it was a postcard.

"I can do this," she said to herself. Today was her walkthrough day of the property. She thought it had been a good omen that the day was cool. She'd put on a tan dress with wide straps, no sleeves and stopped at her knee so she could get in and out of the car. She had chosen this dress because it allowed her to stretch her legs, as she wasn't sure how long the walk was going to be. She'd put on a pair of white flats that she always found comfortable. The realtor had told her it would be a long walk to survey the place and Elizabeth had tried to dress in a cool, professional way that still allowed her to do the survey.

"Are you going to sit in that car all day long?" Henry Jenkins was standing at the gate to the house. "Do you need any help?"

It was on the tip of her tongue to say, "No, I don't need any help from the likes of you." She could see how telling her prospective landlord to go away may not be the best way to start off the working relationship. She stepped out of the car and thought, *so much for the realtor earning his keep.*

Once again, Henry Jenkins was a man who needed to be appreciated when she saw him. She wondered if any ventilation was happening with those jeans. From where she was standing, they looked like they hugged every curve of his muscular legs.

"You're going to be my guide?"

Henry ran his hand through his hair and then smiled. "I'll be happy to be your guide anytime you need one." He pushed open the little gate to the front of the house. "Come on in."

She wanted to reply with something witty and sophisticated. Instead, she just closed the door to her car and walked in. In her mind, she thought, *this is how all the horror movies went. A woman who has no family and friends goes to a small town to start over, and the crazy is some gorgeous guy who just happens to have an isolated place.* She was internally shaking her head with the whole scenario.

Who was she kidding? Henry Jenkins made her uncomfortable. Or maybe the truthful answer would be he made her very comfortable. He had managed to pique her interest as a woman, and because she was still in her, I-don't-trust-men phase, this piquing was not welcome.

She wasn't here to marry the man; just use his land. Maybe she was thinking about it all wrong. Maybe he could help her learn to trust men again period.

After she walked through the door, he looked at her and said, "Please, follow me around the house so we can see the grounds you're considering."

She nodded and then walked behind him.

Goodness, this man looks good from every direction.

"You're awfully quiet. Is there something on my face or back," he asked as he strode forward.

"No, but then I wouldn't expect it," Elizabeth said.

Henry turned and looked at it. "You wouldn't expect it because——"

"Well, for you to have anything on you would suggest you've been doing work on the land, and while I'm not saying it's impossible, it's just that your clothes say it's not probable."

"I'm wounded!" He said, placing his hand by his chest.

Elizabeth couldn't help but smile at the antics. "Ahh, so I'm right; you didn't do anything today."

"I'm not going to answer that. Instead, I'm going to take the high road and change the subject. Nice day for a stroll, don't you think?"

"Yes," she said as she looked around. After they had entered the gate, she saw from one end of the yard to the other, there was a garden of blooming flowers. Then he took her through a house that she barely had time to take in. Moments later, they were in the back of the house and looking at open space.

"The weather is good today too," he said as they both stood in the backyard.

"Yeah, I guess."

"Is that all you're going to say today?"

"I didn't realize this was a meet and greet. I thought I was here to get a tour of the land. Can you do that?"

"You know I think that's your problem, you're always jumping to conclusions," Henry said.

Elizabeth stopped and put her hands on her hips. "Are you serious?"

Henry turned to face her. "I'm just saying, think about yesterday. There I was trying to help save your dog and—"

She tried breathing through her nose, hoping she wouldn't reach out and strangle him.

"Smiley wasn't lost, and if you had just left him alone, then I wouldn't have thought you were stealing him!"

"I read how people can't admit they're wrong because it makes them feel vulnerable. I want you to know that I respect your space and if you don't want to admit you were wrong, I'll let it go, so you can keep your safe space."

She grabbed the side of her dress and bunched it in her hand. If she held on to her side, she wouldn't reach for him. They hadn't even begun to view the property, and she was two seconds from killing him. She had to think of the dogs and how this land would help them. Baring Mr. In-Tune-With-His-Feelings, the surrounding land was amazing. They let an awkward silence settle between them as they continued on. She walked by Henry and started on what looked like a path further into the property.

Everywhere she looked there seemed to be flatlands covered in green grass. There were no barriers as far as she could see, just space. She could image putting in trees to break up the landscape. She might even think about environmentally safe dog houses and pens. When Elizabeth looked at the land, she saw possibilities.

As she walked the path, she could see she was wrong about the barriers. There was a copse of trees ahead. She looked over her shoulder to see Henry following behind.

"Is this the only space like this?"

"You mean with trees? Yes. Keep going, you'll find something else."

She picked up her pace until she was finally past the first set of trees. Inside there was a paradise where it appeared there was a small pond in the center of the trees.

"How did this happen?"

Henry walked ahead of her and opened his arms. "When my dad was young and still believed in love, he did this for my mother. It was before I was born, but it's been here ever since."

"I was told the property had been abandoned and that it was basically just an open field with no farming potential. I didn't know it had history to it," Elizabeth said in hushed tones. "I just wanted a place to start over with my dogs."

"This place has been in Jenkins' hands for over seventy years. Any Jenkins man who has come here and stayed, has never found love or he has destroyed it," Henry said solemnly.

Elizabeth looked at him and saw more. "Is that why you're here? To see if you can get past that stigma?" she asked.

Henry looked around the clearing. She saw the wind blow through his hair, and he put his hands in his jean pockets. With the fit of those pants she would have bet there wasn't space to do so, but she was proved wrong.

"I'd like to think that I've learned enough to be better. I want to be able to see my son grow up. I took the first steps in getting back my family's land so I could do this deal with you."

She nodded and looked around as well before settling back on him. "I think that you're making a good effort."

Elizabeth thought about how much history must be here. She thought about the rumors that she had idly heard at breakfast that very morning in the hotel. People spoke about how the Jenkins boy was trying to do right after leaving his wife and kid here in Sweet Blooms.

"Sweet Blooms seems like a very traditional sort of place," she began, "and you should be able to find your place amongst the old-timers if for no other reason than you came home and stayed."

Henry smiled. "I'm hoping they feel the same way. I have to meet the council this week."

Elizabeth's ears perked up. "Why does it matter? You do own the property, right? I mean, you're not wasting my time, are you?"

Henry held his hands out in front of him. "Calm down, you're jumping again. I legally own all of the property, just like your grant stipulated. But small towns are a different animal. I need to run it by the council—even though I don't really have to."

"That makes no sense!"

"It doesn't now, but wait until you want some work done. A permit or license can take way longer than it needs to when you've offended the council by not asking their opinion."

Elizabeth shook her head. "I guess I don't get all the workings of a town yet. I guess they might want to know why you've come back as well."

Henry gave her a sad grin. "I left home and made some money. I have enough investments to live comfortably. Not enough to support the land but enough that I wouldn't want for anything if I lived a certain way. What it all comes down to is I want to come home. When time is creeping up on you, you realize that home, no matter the drama, is still the place you want to be."

Elizabeth shrugged. "You've got me there. I wouldn't know how to relate. I'm alone, and I've never had a home like that."

Henry chuckled. "There are some days when I think you might be the luckier one of us two. Sometimes coming home means facing old wounds."

A bright cardinal that landed on a nearby branch caught Elizabeth's attention. It chirped as if it knew it was being watched. She didn't know if what Henry was saying was true about home, but she knew she was trying to create one for her and the dogs.

"So you're going to meet with the council so you can smooth over some of those wounds?" she asked.

"I'm going to give it a try." He started to walk and motioned for her to follow him. She could see to the other side of the pond where a gully had a little river trickling through it.

"If you follow this river, it will take you to the Cade's property. The hill isn't steep, but you have to be careful going down it. The Cade property is about two miles along the river. This river will dry up during some seasons, so you'll have to dig deep to find a water line to fill the wells." He walked towards a rock and offered her a seat. "We can take a moment to breathe."

"Thanks." She took off her shoes to let her feet air

out and wiggled her toes. When she looked up, she saw Henry sitting on a nearby boulder, throwing stones along the top of the water. When he reached over the side of the boulder to retrieve a stone, she could see the muscles beneath his shirt flex and bulge as he did. When he sat back up and skidded the rocks over the water, she noticed a scar or two on his hands. He had man-hands. Hands that had seen work. Elizabeth would have never thought she was the kind of woman to notice a man's hands, but Henry's were manly.

Trying to focus on some type of intelligent conversation, she cleared her throat. "You were married before?"

"Yup."

"I imagine it must be a huge adjustment to see this place being repurposed. Were you planning on staying during the renovation?"

"I was planning on staying on longer than just the renovation."

Elizabeth looked at him as he skidded the stones. He hadn't stopped since the conversation began. Was he even affected by what they were discussing? It was true that the land was large enough for both of them to live on, but she hadn't expected him to stay. He was the kind of man she would be looking for to leave. She thought that if he had left the marriage and left his home what would make him stay on here after everything had been fixed?

She didn't need him to do anything, and she didn't want him to be a part of the everyday build or design. She didn't think she could trust any man again after her ex betrayed her. She definitely didn't think she could trust a man who had a track record of leaving and quitting. One day she knew she would be able to get past the mistrust, but it would be with someone who wasn't so attractive. Someone she had a better chance of connecting with and keeping. Elizabeth never sugar-coated the truth with herself. It would be with someone she felt safe with.

"Animal Rescue, has it always been your passion?" he asked.

"No, not always but it turned into that over the last three years."

"Always rescue dogs?"

"I actually started out with strays and the homeless."

"I think there's a story in there," he teased.

"Maybe for another day but not today. Needless to say I discovered that strays provide a lot of emotional support for the homeless and the elderly. When their owners pass on its hard to rehome the pets. A lot of them are old and have medical issues. If it's not that you'll find a lot of stray pets who were living on the street have a hard time living in a home."

"So you've decided to save them all?"

Elizabeth looked at him and noticed he wasn't skipping rocks anymore. "It's something like that. What I'll say is it's a debt I want to repay."

"Do you have a name?"

Elizabeth smiled. "Yes, it's going to be called Sweet Inspirations."

Henry gave her a side look.

"Each one of these pets was someone's inspiration to keep going and get up the next day."

Henry smiled. "I never thought about it like that."

Elizabeth nodded and smiled and then her common sense came rushing back to her. What was she doing here? It was time to put some distance between her and Henry. He was entirely too likable.

"So what else did you plan on doing next in your life? Opening up a company? Finding a way to make more money here in Sweet Blooms? I know you said you wanted to come home, but certainly you need to do something so you don't get bored."

"I don't think I'll be doing any of those things any time soon. I just want to be home for a while."

"You don't think you'll be bored and miss the thrill of making money?"

Henry shook his head. "The thrill of making money isn't a thrill after you do it the first five times."

Elizabeth laughed. "You mean you're bored with making money? Who says that unless they're a millionaire?"

Henry chuckled. "I'm definitely not a millionaire but making money isn't all it's cracked up to be when you're alone."

"I appreciate your help with the land, but I don't want to hem you in here," she said. "The dogs are old and need stability in their lives. They need to know who will be here and who won't."

"I like dogs. Like I said, I don't plan on leaving. I'm trying to make some changes in my life."

Henry looked so sincere as he talked to her. She heard that sincerity, and it seeped into her chest and wrapped around her heart. Those words were the words of a man trying and all of a sudden, he was more. Her awareness of him was more than just a person she had just met. Her attraction was moving from his physicality to making him into a person worth knowing. This was a forbidden road.

Elizabeth knew better than to stay around any man that she was attracted to. Historically, she had poor taste and no matter how down to earth and sincere Henry seemed, she knew it was a sham. She stood up and brushed off her dress.

"Well, I think I've seen enough. It's time to go back. I hope you find what you're looking for Henry."

She saw the opening to the trail and started going towards it.

"Elizabeth?"

She stopped and plastered a smile on her face before turning to him.

"Since I'm going to be here anyway, what do you think about me helping out with the dogs?"

It sounded perfect. Here was an attractive man asking her if he could help out with what was now her life passion. But in the back of her mind, little details kept coming to the surface. For one, he seemed to change his mind a lot. If he did it in a marriage and with a child, how long before helping out with dogs would grow old. Everyone loved dogs in the beginning, but when it came time to do the thankless work of cleaning kennels, brushing teeth and combing crotchety dogs, it wasn't so much fun anymore.

"Thank you. It means a lot that you would consider it," she told him with her smile firmly in place. "It's way more time consuming than you may think, though."

He crossed his arms over his chest. "What exactly does that mean?"

Elizabeth looked at Henry and blinked twice before blurting out. "It means the answer is no."

Henry took a step back as if she had hit him. The friendly, approachable man was gone and in his place was someone different. "You don't think I understand what kind of commitment it takes?"

"I think that's being generous. I don't know if you know commitment at all."

Elizabeth hated all kinds of confrontation. She definitely didn't want to start on the wrong foot with the man who owned the land she was using. However, she wasn't really good at lying either. If she let Henry help and he did good work that would be great for her. She could hire fewer people and save some money on her yearly budget. The downside was when Henry discovered it was work and his good nature was done, he would leave, and she'd have to scramble to find someone to help out at Inspirations.

Letting out a sigh and seeing him standing still, she thought the best thing she could do was go home.

"Listen, I think it's best if I see myself back. Maybe we'll be able to regroup and rethink things then."

She didn't wait for a response, she turned and left. She had imagined this day ending a lot of ways but this definitely was not one of them. Day one and the potential tenant says the landlord is a flake.

Three

One of the things Henry missed when he left home was the farm work. He knew a lot of people who thought he couldn't stand to do it, but they were wrong. He loved the idea that he could do something and see the fruit of that work right away. At the back of the house there was a garden that was closed up. The only reason it was even still viable was because Hannah came by to tend it. Eventually, he'd have to get someone to tend to the garden on a regular basis or cover it up with grass seed.

Beyond the garden was a small stable. It was big enough to hold four horses but right now it had two in it. Two horses were more than enough for Henry.

The horses were boarding at his place while their stables were being refitted. He woke up at the crack of dawn to get the feed ready for the horses and make sure he had hay to put in the stalls after he had raked them out. He enjoyed these mornings. It was just him and the sweat of his brow. These mornings helped him to think things through and most important to keep in shape. City living could put a few pounds on you if you weren't careful.

Normally, he would lose himself in the work, but today he couldn't find that peaceful place at all. He emptied the bag of grain in the trough as if he wanted to strangle the grain bag. When he began to clean out the stall, he used the rake like a weapon and attacked the old hay. It was enough to make the mare next to him eye him carefully over the divider. He didn't have to wonder what the reason was. He knew he was still thinking about Elizabeth's words from yesterday.

He wanted to say she'd been mean to make those assumptions. However, there had been many a night he'd beaten himself up over the irresponsibility of his youth and his shortsightedness. He was fortunate that Hannah was the woman she was; otherwise, his selfishness could have cost him being in his son's life. More than likely, what made Elizabeth's words cut deep was the fact he liked her. Elizabeth had been the first woman he could tease and joke with. Just thinking about her getting all riled up when he said he saved her dog brought a smile to his mouth.

He put the rake against the wall and then unrolled the hay. He knew he would live with the stain of his irresponsibility. He didn't expect people to forgive him or forget that he hadn't been mature enough to handle a wife and child. Every day he was grateful that Hannah had been able to step up to the plate and help their son be the great person he was today.

At the same time, he didn't want to be branded a flake for the rest of his life. Logically he knew he was supposed to move on. Emotionally he felt as though this would always be used against him in a relationship or used against him to judge the man he was today.

He wondered if he would ever be able to do enough to live down his past. He didn't know if he could, but he was determined to try. Before Elizabeth, he had been sure he could do it. He would ignore the gossips and just go forward. All of that resolve went by the wayside when he saw the look of disapproval in Elizabeth's eyes yesterday. He had felt low, and worse, he had agreed with her. He had just put fresh hay in the stall and was trying to decide if he was done beating himself up for his past when he heard the horse neigh, and he looked at the barn door. Standing there in a purple, short sleeve shirt and a purple and white, floral skirt was the woman in his thoughts.

He could smell the light floral scent in the air. The horses in the barn fidgeted from the newcomer but seemed to calm down as soon as they ascertained she was no threat. She walked into the barn and he imagined what she must see. An old building with a step to a second floor on one side and horse stalls on the other wall. The tools were on the wall if they weren't being used and the floor was littered with hay.

While the horses had decided she wasn't a threat that didn't mean they didn't watch her as she came into the barn. He had to admit he was just as enthralled, even if it was for a different reason. He found himself fascinated with the sway of her skirt and how the flowers seemed to move with the natural grace of her body.

There was nothing exotic about her. He'd seen women in skirts, sandals and short sleeve shirts before. But everything looked different on Elizabeth. Maybe it was the confidence she brought with her. It was a subtle mystery of this woman who projected so much strength, yet was wrapped in a package that said she was delicate.

She was a woman that a man would take a second and third look at.

He thought she would turn towards him, but after a few moments, Elizabeth actually went to touch the tools on the wall and looked up steps that were on the other side. He thought she was just making him wait, but after a moment he realized this wasn't some waiting-woman trick, she was looking around the barn as if she had never seen one.

Henry turned back to the task at hand. He had been spreading the hay for about five minutes when he felt that tingly feeling on the back of his neck. He thought about trying to ignore her, but he wasn't that man. She'd told him what she really thought, and even if he didn't like it, he had to respect her for voicing her opinion and telling him to his face. Henry had been thinking that he had been guilty too of jumping the gun. She looked so delicate and put together, but maybe he had made the assumption that she would jump at his offer because he was the strong man to help the little woman. He shook his head and turned to face her. Yeah, maybe he had made some assumptions himself.

Henry was pro 'give every a chance to every woman' but a nice pair of legs, a strong personality and a woman willing to defend a dog caught his attention. When he wiped his hands on his pants and made sure the rake was against the wall and not on the floor, he was ready to face her.

If he was ready, she was waiting. He looked right into her eyes. He didn't know what to expect today, so he folded his arms across his stomach and waited.

Elizabeth looked at him and then the barn. "I didn't know you still did this kind of thing."

He waited for the next quip. He knew people thought that way about it him, but for some reason, knowing that she had looked at him and just seen less, caused him to keep a blank face and just hope for this to be over soon.

She threw her hands up in the air. "Listen," she said exasperated. "I shouldn't have said what I said yesterday. You're a special case. You're my landlord, and at that moment it sounded like you were also asking to be my employee, and I make quick decisions about my employees. I realize now though, that I might not need to do that with my landlord."

He looked at her, shifting from foot to foot and taking several breaths.

"Are you trying to say you're sorry?"

"I'm not saying I'm sorry! I'm saying I was rude!"

Henry smiled. "Ahh, well, that makes all the sense now."

"It should. I was taught if you don't have something nice to say, to say nothing. I broke that rule with you."

"Wow, this is hard for you. Fortunately, I'm a forgiving man, and I want you to know. You don't have to say sorry to me for me to know that's what your heart truly wants to say."

"Kick rocks!" she grumbled. "Uh! Not that I'm suggesting you do mindless things like kick rocks all day. I mean, it's an expression that—"

"I know the expression, Elizabeth."

"Great. Well, to your other question. If you have time after doing this work, we can go over the schedule to see where you would want to work and when you would have time."

"Does that mean I get the first choice of the best positions since you were rude and all?"

"No! It means that you get to choose if you want to go through orientation with a group or just me."

Henry smiled. "How could I pass up an offer like that?"

"Remember, it's always about the dogs."

"I get that. Do you think there is something you're going to show me that I don't already know?"

Elizabeth grinned. "We all think we know something about taking care of our pets. When you get into it, you may find it's a steeper learning curve than you thought."

"I think I can keep pace."

"It can't be easy living in town with your ex. Or having your ex marry a super-hot, rich guy."

Henry chuckled. "When you say it like that, it has a whole different feel to it."

Elizabeth sighed. "What I'm trying to say is, I know it can't be easy living in a town where everyone believes in marriage being forever. I try to give everyone a chance, and my own issues got in the way. I didn't mean to take it out on you."

Henry looked at her as she spoke, and he nodded. "Thanks," he said with a smile. She turned around and walked out of the barn. "Hey Elizabeth, what did you come for?"

"To set things right. I mean, it was bothering me, so I decided to help us both. See you later."

Henry watched her go. That skirt played peek a boo with long, firm legs. Oh yes, Elizabeth Butler was definitely the type of woman to make a man take a second look.

There are no secrets in a small town. Everyone knew that Henry Jenkins was going to the council to update them on the land usage. Elizabeth thought it was a bit dramatic. She had already signed the papers. Henry had already signed the papers, and her dogs would be arriving soon. Today was one of those practices that happened in small towns that she wasn't sure she could get her arms around. It reminded her too much of judgment.

After what she had said to Henry yesterday, she was the last one to be critical of people being judgy.

While the council meeting was in the courthouse it wasn't a lavish courthouse or even a semblance of anything legal. The council room was just that, a large room that could hold about sixty people. She was told that hadn't been done since the town had to take a vote if they would allow the high school kids to decorate a house using the color red. While the town wanted the kids to explore their creativity, no one wanted to encourage a house of ill repute. Elizabeth had heard Agnes, the local gossip and member of the town council, at the coffee shop while she explained her logic. "First the house would be red, then there would be parties at all times of night. Before you knew it, it would be a house of ill repute corrupting the youth!"

Elizabeth had to leave after that comment this morning. However, she did hear as she was paying that everyone was saying that today's hearing might attract just as many people since the Jenkins boy was gonna be there.

Elizabeth saw Henry standing in front of a podium. He was dressed in a white shirt and blue tie, with dark blue slacks. He looked like he had just stepped out of an office. Even though she knew this was already done, she could feel a bit of trepidation as he stood at the podium.

She had been referred to Sweet Blooms. The first person she had met was Mayor Mason, who was all for the idea of a senior dog retreat. The mayor had assured Elizabeth that the town was business-friendly. It looked like Sweet Blooms was business-friendly, but it didn't forget a person's history. This meeting seemed like a meeting to judge Henry.

Elizabeth could see Henry shifting from foot to foot and flexing his hands on the perimeter of the podium. Then the council members came in from the side, and the room which was packed with murmuring people began to quiet. When the Mayor had told her the council was eclectic, Elizabeth thought that was in regard to age, but she could see they all looked like unique characters.

She saw Henry look over his shoulder at the crowd, and like a magnet, he found Elizabeth in the group. She smiled at him and gave him the thumbs up. Henry nodded, and that made a couple of the women turn and look at Elizabeth. One older woman looked at Elizabeth and harrumphed. Elizabeth looked around the room, and she wished she had gotten a seat closer to the front. She knew he could do this. After the way she treated him, and he still talked to her, Elizabeth felt as though this council thing would be easy.

The mayor clapped her hands, and everyone was at attention. Elizabeth wanted to laugh; it was more like a teacher calling everyone's attention than any kind of council meeting she'd ever been to.

"I can see all of you came out to hear what Henry Jenkins would like to do on his land. We will take care of other matters first."

The mayor sat at the middle of the table. There were a total of five of them, so the mayor had two on each side of her. She picked up the papers that were in front of her and her dangling earrings swayed with the movement. The mayor was definitely dressed corporate casual in a crème colored top and brown slacks. Her hair was up in a bun which made her look both severe and matronly. A horrifying combination.

"The first item on the agenda are the houses at the end of Flower Street that are under construction. With so many new businesses and families coming, we need to build more homes. Unfortunately, as they are being built, unsavories are finding their way to them," the mayor stated.

"I don't know why we keep saying unsavories, we all know it's the high school kids trying to find a hideaway to do the deed!" commented an older woman. The woman was dressed in black from head to toe. She was in her late seventies, judging from the veins coming through paper-thin skin on her hands. She kept moving one of the glasses of water that was set at each seating on the stage.

Elizabeth saw the mayor close her eyes, and then a smile showed on her face. "Now Agnes, all things that are going awry in the town are not the kids' fault."

"Are too."

"Agnes, please try to hold your comments until it's your turn. I think we have some travelers who have fallen on hard times or are passing through."

A woman with blonde hair pulled up into a messy bun, and a red dress with a low neckline and ample cleavage leaned over to see the mayor. When she leaned forward, Elizabeth could swear several of the men leaned with her. "I think we need to send some law enforcement to patrol the situation."

"I've been saying that about your choice of clothing for years, and no one has listened," murmured Agnes.

The mayor turned to her right and looked at Agnes. "Agnes, if you don't have anything to contribute in a positive fashion regarding the issue at hand, I'll have you send in your responses, and a representative will read them for you."

Agnes sniffed and then rearranged her water. Elizabeth wondered if any of them noticed the little black discs on the table, to the side of each person. It was a microphone, and it was very sensitive to all of their conversations.

The mayor looked to her right and spoke to the woman whose cleavage was clinging to the dress. "Clarissa, I've spoken to the chief, and he will be sending some extra people out there at different times. I'm hoping this helps with the vagrancy."

"I'm not one to encourage early marriage or teen moms, but I think the kids need to have a public, secret place to go and be kids," said a woman who was next to Clarissa.

Elizabeth looked around, and everyone in the audience was enthralled. While Elizabeth thought it was one step from laughing out loud, she could also see it was serious business.

Agnes tapped the table, and the mayor nodded in her direction. "I haven't had to ask to speak since my dad passed. Anyway, I think Loretta is right. We need a public, secret place for the kids to be caught before they do the wrong thing."

Then the only man on the board sighed and spoke.

"I think you ladies have far too much time to think about who's doing what where. I think that suggests there is an entirely different kind of problem with the older women in the town," he leaned forward and smiled at Clarissa. "Not all the women, but everyone will know who they are. The chief is going to drive by. Let's wait a week, and we'll find out where the new spot is."

Just when other people were about to jump in, the mayor clapped her hand.

"We'll be putting to a vote if the chief should do patrolling. If you think yes, raise your hand. Jerry, can you count the hands?"

Elizabeth watched the hands go up, and a few seconds later, Jerry spoke.

"It was more than half as long as we agree it's a go."

There were some more rumblings going on, but then the Mayor nodded and clapped.

"That took a little longer than I thought, so we'll move on to the Jenkins piece."

Henry tapped the microphone at the podium and cleared his throat.

"Thank you for seeing me," he said.

"Boy, you know we'd hear you out. It's true you're a Jenkins, but you're still a part of Sweet Blooms," Agnes said.

The mayor gave Agnes another look. Elizabeth shook her head. She couldn't even imagine being the mayor up there. Henry approached the table and gave out a sheet of paper. He looked just as at ease in those business clothes as he had in his jeans in the barn. In both situations, Elizabeth had to admit there was an extra bit of confidence, strength, and purpose when he walked. He held his head up high and smiled at all of them.

He explained the land would be used for rescue dogs. He explained how the grant would pay for it for the next three years. At the end of the three years, he would reapply. By the time he gave out all of the papers with the pictures of the dogs on them, everyone was nodding how great the idea was and how unexpected it was that a Jenkins would do it.

"I can see you planned this," Mayor Mason said. "However, I do have to ask. Knowing your background in real estate and that you have been and still are successful in this field, I'm a little surprised that you've gone this route instead of finding a realtor or someone to build a mall on it and bringing us that proposal."

Elizabeth was taken back by the direct question. She thought the question bordered on rude, but who was she to say?

Henry cleared his throat and then turned so that he saw the council and the crowd.

"I'm sure everyone here knows me or my name. My thought is I'd like to keep my family land and settle here. I'm not looking to make a dollar, I have a couple of those. Not as many as Adam Cade, but a few."

The comment brought about a couple of laughs and someone called out, "None of us have as many dollars as Adam Cade!"

The mayor clapped and brought the attention back to her. "So this move would be permanent?"

Henry nodded. "Yes, ma'am."

Agnes cleared her throat, and the mayor nodded.

"Well, his father was slicker than a snake. I think you mean good, but I'm gonna wait for a spell before I start believing you've knocked the dust off of your shoes."

"The way you women nag maybe he's got the better sense to go," Jerry grumbled.

Elizabeth looked at Henry as he stood there. She didn't see his expression change at all. All the while, the council went back and forth amongst themselves over the history of Jenkins men. Still, Henry didn't move. In that moment, as she watched him stand up against the town and not lash back, she was determined to give him more of a chance than the town was.

With a clap, the mayor ended the chatter. She turned to Henry and gave him a nod but then turned to address the crowd.

"The council has decided to let Henry Jenkins open Sweet Inspirations on the Jenkins land."

Four

Henry couldn't get out of the council room fast enough. He felt like a politician, before he could leave he had to shake some hands, reminisce over what was, and he even kissed a baby to prove a Jenkins man could. He looked everywhere for the one friendly face he wanted to see, but she was nowhere to be found.

He knew what he was going into when he agreed to the council meeting. The difference was she was there. It felt different to have someone in his corner. Someone who he knew was cheering him on.

Then when it was over and he didn't see her, he was disappointed. She hadn't promised to stay, but he had thought she would. He was still nursing the regret when he made it to the parking lot and saw his truck. More importantly, she was leaning against the door.

"I thought you knew how to get out of those things. I've been waiting here forever," Elizabeth said.

Her words spread through him, and even though he was frustrated and angry, it seemed manageable now.

"If I had known I had such a lovely lady waiting for me, I would have made it out of there much quicker," he replied. He looked around. "Did you bring your chariot my lady?"

"I did but it's a rental and it seems a perk of being in a small town is the hotel will pick up my car, because they know everybody."

"Then let's be on our way," he said.

He opened the door to his truck, and she walked to the other side. By the time she got in, the engine was going, and he was ready to roll out.

"Where are we going?"

"We're going home," he replied. When she didn't say anything and he started driving, he hadn't realized that he had been holding his breath. She didn't start a conversation. She didn't turn on the radio. She just rolled down the window, and he could see her hair blowing in the wind.

He was used to people whispering behind his back. Henry grew up not having his own name but being a Jenkin's man. In Sweet Blooms, he lived under the shadow of his father's alcoholism. When he was younger, all the things he did that teens did, the silly things to impress his friends, and a girl, was attributed to his bad start of being a Jenkins.

He'd left Sweet Blooms to prove himself. When he went to New York, no one knew he was a Jenkins boy. He'd made his way there and managed to put away a little money. He had to prove to himself he was more than just his father's reputation. The issue seemed to be when he was away from home, people respected him. When he came back, it was like he had never left.

"Why do I even let it bother me?" he muttered as he drove the truck towards the house. When they arrived, neither one of them moved.

"You know I was born in this house," he said.

Elizabeth turned towards him. "You mean you were conceived in this house?" she said.

Henry laughed and looked at a confused Elizabeth. "No *born* in this house. As in, the second-floor bedroom."

"Wow, I thought that only happened in the movies. Was it a snowstorm?"

"No, every firstborn, male Jenkins has been born in this house for the last sixty years."

"That must be a hard position to fill. Fall in love with a Jenkins and then you have to have his baby at the house?"

"It sounds odd when you say it."

"It sounds dangerous."

"I can think of a lot of things that would have been more dangerous."

Elizabeth shook her head. "This sale is still a hard one."

"Okay, well, I had good times here. It's true they were few and far between, but I had some."

"Okay, let me have it. Tell me a happy time."

Henry thought about it. "The time my dad took me fishing. I never liked putting the bait on the hook when I was smaller. My dad would tell me if I closed my eyes and thought about the fish I wanted to catch, then the right bait would jump on the hook."

Elizabeth laughed. "That would be very accommodating of everyone if that was the case."

Henry looked out his window and at the house. "My dad had already baited several hooks, and when I closed my eyes, he'd pull one out, and I'd fish. I was young then. I thought he could still do miracles then."

"I don't know how happy that is, but okay."

"Okay, Missy, you think of a happy time from your childhood."

"Okay, the day I got adopted was the best day ever. Everyone had said I wouldn't get picked and that I was too old. I was seven. Anyway, the Butlers saw me and adopted me. It was the best day of my childhood."

Henry really looked at Elizabeth and realized he knew nothing about her. She might have jumped the gun and said some things that were off-color, but he had judged her too. He thought she had never had any real hardship. He shook his head and laughed to himself. He had judged her the same way he had been judged. He looked back at her and shrugged.

"Okay, you win."

He could see that she was about to answer when a small brown car drove up to his drive and parked in front of him. A man got out of the car, and Henry thought he looked more like a beetle than a man. He might have been five foot six, but he was hunched over, shrinking him to five foot two. He had on black glasses and he wore dark pants with a white, long sleeve shirt which had large sweat stain under the arms.

Henry was going to tell Elizabeth to stay while he met the stranger, but she was already out and in front.

"Hello Mr. Zecky, it's me, Elizabeth Butler. I didn't expect you today."

The beetle man looked at Elizabeth, pushed up his glasses, and then stepped towards her with a smile. He must have been all of sixty-five. Whatever they were asking him to do, it was too much. Sweet Blooms was filled with older adults who were fit and in their prime. Mr. Zecky looked like he might not make it to the next appointment, with his slow gait and stilted movements.

"Ms. Butler. I'm actually en route to another land space, but I wanted to see if all was going well."

Henry couldn't hear beyond that because Elizabeth was closer to Mr. Beetle. When she made it to his side, they both had their heads together and then laughed. The beetle man actually looked around Elizabeth at him and then nodded. Elizabeth turned around with a large smile on her face. He wasn't sure what had been said, but whatever it was, it was making Elizabeth nervous. Her smile was in place, but it didn't reach her eyes.

Mr. Beetle held out his hand to Henry. "So you are the generous Henry Jenkins," he said. Henry grabbed Mr. Beetle's hand, and he had to stop himself from pulling back from the sweaty palm. "I'm Lionel Zecky from the grant board. It's good to meet you."

"Same."

Mr. Zecky's hand almost slid out of Henry's. Henry once again plastered on a smile and did his best to wipe his hands by putting them in his pockets.

"Mr. Jenkins, I'm so happy you decided to donate the property. A lot of men wouldn't be so generous," he said.

Henry looked at Elizabeth again. Her smile was in place, but he thought he saw her swallow and look right past him.

"Elizabeth makes a compelling case for the dogs," he said.

"She must, but I understand how these things go." Mr. Zecky said, adding a wink to his statement. Henry looked at Elizabeth, and she had her eyes closed, and her lips pursed together.

Then Elizabeth interjected. "Mr. Zecky, we're not ready today as we don't have the plan, so why don't we set up another time for us to go over how the grant money will be allocated."

Mr. Zecky smiled and then reached out and patted Elizabeth on the shoulder.

"No worries, I understand, my dear. Believe it or not, I was once young too. Young love is a powerful thing."

Henry heard the statement and then looked at Elizabeth. There was definitely some subtext he was missing. Elizabeth seemed so eager for Mr. Zecky to go, and none of the comments were adding up.

"Young love?" Henry said.

Then Mr. Zecky looked at Elizabeth and patted her on the arm before turning to Henry.

"I know the two of you are trying to keep this a secret, and I told Ms. Butler that I would use the utmost discretion. But she had told me about your relationship. I mean, it's not every day the grant gets an application that says 'my fiancé is giving me some land, and I want to use it to create a home for senior, abandoned dogs.'"

Five

Elizabeth trailed behind Henry as he walked Mr. Zecky to his car. She felt like she was on death row, and there wasn't a thing she could do about it. Any moment she expected Henry to say something. To deny that there was any relationship. Instead, as they walked Mr. Zecky gave all sorts of wise information to Henry on how to be in a relationship with a woman he must adore.

The good news was Henry didn't immediately tell Mr. Zecky that they weren't involved. In fact, she was very impressed with how Henry went right along and acted as if nothing earth-shattering had been said. Henry nodded respectfully at every suggestion Mr. Zecky gave him. Elizabeth supposed that even Mr. Zecky could see that Henry was tense.

Looking over Henry's shoulder. "Well, I'll let the two of you get back to getting to know each other."

Elizabeth came to stand beside Henry when she called out to Mr. Zecky.

"Mr. Zecky, let me know where you want to meet next time, and I'll come to meet you."

Mr. Zecky waved her off. "No, no, my dear, it's nothing. I think I'll do this review in person. You know

I spend a lot of time in the air on planes, and it would be great to be able to do a review in person. This assignment allows me to see a place close up instead of watching it in a skype view."

Just as she was about to follow Mr. Zecky to the car and try to talk some sense into him, she felt an arm go about her waist and stop her.

"Hey," she hissed under her breath to Henry.

"Oh I think I'll hold on until Mr. Zecky leaves so we can discuss this newfound, young love we have."

Elizabeth looked at Henry and decided to do what she had always done. Follow her gut. She leaned into Henry and then smiled at Mr. Zecky.

"I know how important privacy is to Henry. I want to thank you, Mr. Zecky, for keeping our engagement a secret."

She waited for him to correct her. If he did it now, then she could just go back to the hotel and then try something else, but she wasn't going to be dangling on a string, wondering if he was going along with this or not. Elizabeth thought to force his hand now so he'd agree or disagree in front of Mr. Zecky. She didn't hear him say anything, but his hand did seem to tighten a bit around her waist.

The things you could tell from an arm about the waist. She could now confirm, Henry Jenkins did work out, or he just had great muscles in his arm. When his arm had first gone around her waist, she had stiffened, but then it looked like Mr. Zecky took a little longer looking at her in Henry's arms.

When she relaxed into his arm that was when she started to notice some things. Henry's hand was warm. Not sweaty hot like Mr. Zecky but warm, as the warmth from his arm seeped into her waist and wove itself through her body. Then when Mr. Zecky stopped again before getting in his car, because he needed direction, Henry started to move his fingers on her side until it was like he was caressing her hip. After a couple of strokes, it seemed like her clothes were in the way instead of helping her. It was the slamming of Mr. Zecky's door and watching him drive away that broke the spell of being in Henry's arm. Then she felt him rest his chin atop of her head and he whispered.

"Do you think you should tell me something?" he asked in a smooth voice that seemed to seep into her bones. She heard his words and all things being equal; he didn't sound anywhere as upset as she thought he would.

Elizabeth knew that he was trying to start anew. After attending the council meeting, she knew it was going to be a hard road that would be watched by everyone in the town; if he had really made a new turn or not.

Elizabeth knew she wasn't any good at playing dumb, but she didn't want to leave any venue unexplored.

"Was there something in particular, you wanted me to bring you up to speed on?"

She could feel him take a deep breath behind her and she waited, hoping against hope that he would leave this topic alone, but she should have known better. She should have had more faith in the fact that the only luck she had, was bad luck.

"So when were you going to tell me we were engaged?"

She stepped away from him and looked him in the eye. "Never."

Henry had a rule. If you were going to break-up or deliver bad news, you should do it over dinner. It gave everyone the opportunity to appease themselves with food or dessert as a sort of consolation prize. With that in mind, after Elizabeth had answered him, he nodded toward his truck and said: "Let's go eat."

He could see she was confused by his comment, but he needed to eat before having this conversation. Sweet Blooms was expanding, but the place to go for food was The Banter. Geeta, who was everyone's defacto mom, ran The Banter. At The Banter, you could get a meal that wasn't created with caloric value in mind and waitresses who would tell you the truth about today's special.

Henry knew going to The Banter with Elizabeth would cause some buzz, but at this point, a little gossip buzz might be nothing to deal with in the grand scheme of things. At any rate, what he knew for sure was that if he wanted to get good news or bad, this was the place to do it.

He walked into the diner and saw a couple of empty booths. It might have been noon outside but inside, the dark woods and hanging lights above the booths gave a cozy atmosphere. He guided Elizabeth towards a corner booth. The menus were already on the table, waiting for them to sit down.

He had to admit his hand felt as though it was supposed to be around her waist. She was shapely, and his hand was the exact width to fit at her waist.

She always seemed to have on a more colorful dress than the time before. Her clothes were bright like she was. He noticed she liked dresses that were loose, and when a breeze would come by, the material would hug her outline giving subtle hints to the woman beneath. Elizabeth didn't know it, but she had a sensuality that came with being her own woman. Henry always found a woman who was comfortable being herself more attractive than a woman who needed to have the latest beauty trend.

Henry knew he had been deliberately avoiding relationships. He wasn't attracted to just any woman. He liked women who were confident and had a clear idea about what they wanted out of life. Even now, when he was pretty sure that Elizabeth had taken some liberties with her application, he was on the fence. On the one hand he was angry with her for not telling him everything. On the other hand, he was impressed at her commitment to finding a way for something that she believed in. He needed food.

The waitress was a woman who looked to be in her early fifties. Her hair was pulled back in a bun, and she had on blue jeans and a t-shirt that said, Welcome to Banter's. She didn't even glance at Henry. Instead, she directed her questions to Elizabeth.

"Would you like to know the prixe fix for lunch or the special, dear?" the waitress asked patiently. It wasn't until the "dear" that Elizabeth seemed to realize that she was talking to her.

"Um, I'll take the lunch special," Elizabeth said and nodded at the waitress.

The waitress turned towards Henry finally. "You'll be getting the number five," she said.

Henry nodded his head.

"Good, that's done any drink?" the waitress asked again looking to Elizabeth,

"Water, please."

"Good," the waitress said and picked up the menus. "Two glasses of water, one special and a number five."

"Well, it's nice to know some things never change," Henry said.

Elizabeth looked at the retreating back of the waitress and then at him. "What was that about?"

"That was Sonja, Loretta's sister. Loretta was one of the members of the council. Sonja has known me all my life. I was hoping since I was trying to make a new start and get a new reputation that the people wouldn't treat me like I haven't changed, but I guess not."

"So you're not upset with the service just that she remembered what you usually get when you're here?" Elizabeth asked.

"Let's just say today was a day to really look around and understand who and what are in my environment," Henry said.

A few moments passed, and Elizabeth squirmed in her seat.

"Listen, Henry, I'm not one to wait for things, so let's go over whatever you'd like to talk about," Elizabeth said.

The water arrived. He took a drink and then looked at Elizabeth across the table.

"I'm torn between being impressed and insulted."

Elizabeth raised an eyebrow. "Which one of those feelings puts me in a better position? Whichever one it is, I support it."

He looked across at her and grinned. "I bet you do."

A few moments later, a short, stout woman came to the table. She had mocha kissed skin, and her hair was wound up on the top of her head. Her Indian heritage was apparent in her features as well as her dress.

Henry stood up and opened his arms, hugging the woman before taking his seat.

The woman held up her hand.

"Henry Jenkins, why does it take you being in town a good two days before you can see me?"

"Geeta, I'm trying to get myself together, and I wanted to make sure I was worthy," Henry said with a smile.

"Boy, you are so slick I'm surprised you can seat in a booth at all," Geeta replied, then turned to Elizabeth.

"You seem like a nice girl with a lot of secrets. I can see those dark circles under your eyes. Whatever it is, let it go. You're too young to be carrying those bags beneath your eyes."

She turned to Henry and put her hands on her hips, which were lost beneath the pullover shirt she had on.

"Henry, what are you doing to fix this?"

"I—"

"I don't want to hear any of that snake-oil speak either. I know you've got a good heart. Not as good as my Jerry, but Jerry is one of a kind. You get to work and do what you can to make this better. Your food will be out soon, so get to work."

Then Geeta turned back to Elizabeth.

"It's good to meet you, child. I hope when I see you next, you're happier. If you need anything, you come here and tell them Geeta is expecting you, and I'll get you fixed up right away."

Henry looked at Elizabeth as Geeta walked away. "I should have warned you, but I'm so used to it I forgot."

"Is she always like that?" Elizabeth asked.

"No, sometimes she's outspoken." Henry looked at Elizabeth as her eyes went wide, and then she began to laugh.

"Well, if nothing else, she definitely clears the air for an honest conversation."

Henry smiled. "Geeta is an integral part of Sweet Blooms and the better part of Jerry. She has a way of listening without judging and doling out common sense without being intrusive."

"Let's get it out of the way. Ask away, Henry."

"Explain to me why Mr. Zecky thinks we are in a relationship?"

"Well, when I went for the grant, they said that it couldn't be owned by multiple people. No problem. That was why I asked if you owned the land."

"Okay."

"Then, as we got closer to the date, Mr. Zecky called me and asked me why my name wasn't on it. When I questioned him, he made it clear that the person who owned the land had to be the one who was running the grant. This opportunity was one of my last options, and it was sent to me via an email. He actually made the assumption that I was engaged to you, and I didn't correct him. He said we'd do the check via email, and I thought it would be fine. I'd still be giving the money to you anyway for the land. What could go wrong?"

"Well, I'll say this. When I decided to come back and try to remake myself, I never thought I'd get scammed. Being on this side of the fence, I can definitely understand why it was hard for people to trust me," Henry said.

Elizabeth sighed. "I know I was wrong, but I thought it wouldn't hurt anyone, and so much good would come from this. I planned on telling Mr. Zecky that it just hadn't worked out with us after I got the grant about a year in. I'm looking for other things, but some grants want to know I have a history managing grant money before they'll even look at me."

Henry tapped his fingers on the tabletop as he digested her tale.

"The only problem is, here in Sweet Blooms I'm trying to get away from the reputation of marrying or engaging women and then leaving them."

An uncomfortable silence was broken when the food arrived. Henry dug in. the number five was a bacon cheeseburger with fries. He was halfway through with his meal when he realized Elizabeth was picking at her chicken fingers and fries.

"Is something wrong? Did you want something else?" he asked.

She looked at him, confused. "I guess I don't understand how you can eat now?"

Henry swallowed the food in his mouth and took a drink of water. "What do you mean?"

"I mean, you need to tell me what you're going to do about this situation."

Henry sat back and looked at her. "I thought we'd address it after we finished." He could see the look of incredulity on her face. "Or not, now might be good."

Elizabeth pushed her plate to the side and then folded her hands on the table. Henry sighed and looked at the rest of his sandwich. He knew it was over. There would be no going back to finish this.

"So let me start by saying, I totally get what you did and why. One of the reasons that I came back to Sweet Blooms is because I was tired of wheeling and dealing. I make money from some investments, but I didn't want to deal with the pace."

"I remember you mentioned some of that by the water."

"I want people to say my name and not use it as a curse or a warning. This situation of yours puts me in a weird position. The truth of it is I have no idea what I'm going to do."

"Are you joking me?"

Henry nodded at Elizabeth and then pulled his sandwich back to eat it. There were only about four bites left; maybe he could finish it.

Elizabeth reached over and pushed his plate to the side.

"Could you please focus on me for a moment," she said.

Henry sighed and looked at the burger. Just when he was trying to plot a way to get it back, he heard Elizabeth. "Check, please."

He dropped his head and looked at his plate.

"Henry, maybe you think this is a joke, but I need an answer on how you're going to play this. It's not just me; it's my animals too. I know this may seem bossy, but how was I to know you had a history of loving them and dumping them in this town? I'm going to my hotel, you can stay while you try to come up with an answer for me."

When Sonja brought the check, Henry got to it first.

"Give me the check," she said in a low tone.

Henry shrugged. "I can't give you the check. I invited you, so I pay. It's a law somewhere. I also didn't finish my food, so I have to leave a bigger tip, that's just Sweet Blooms practice."

Elizabeth stood up. "Thank you for the meal. Let me know what you decide. Until I hear otherwise, I'll assume we are still on track. I know I seem pushy, Henry. In fact, I've been called a lot worse when I am trying to get something, but I didn't mean any harm by it, and I'd appreciate it if you could remember that when you are making this decision."

"I'm hoping I have time to make this decision."

Elizabeth paused. "What?"

"You weren't born in a small town, and you definitely aren't from Sweet Blooms. News travels in towns, quicker than you can put something on the internet."

Elizabeth shook her head. "We both saw him leave, and he was only here for the day. I think you should focus on getting a decision rather than if the town will mysteriously find out."

Henry watched as she left and then nodded to everyone as he took his leave and made it to his truck. He had a couple of problems. The biggest one was he was attracted to the woman who had just set him up to look like the bad guy again. He moved back to Sweet Blooms for the simple life. Being around Elizabeth was going to be anything but simple.

<h1 style="text-align:center">Six</h1>

Two days later, Elizabeth received an invite to Banters. It was a message left for her in the hotel. She braced herself to meet Henry and get his decision. Instead, when she arrived at The Banter Sonja waved at her and told her to go to the room in the back. Elizabeth thought he was being a bit eccentric needing a whole room to tell her no. What did he think? Did he have a vision of her acting out and causing a scene?

As she approached the room, she heard voices and at once became apprehensive. When she opened the door, three heads turned towards her.

"Come in, come in!" One of the women, who was dressed in blue jeans and a pink tee-shirt that said Dream Possible on it, jumped up to shake her hand. "My name is Lydia. I'm the one who left you the message for you at your hotel. The other two women here are Clarissa, who you've met before on the council, and Daisy, who is neighbors with Henry."

"Hello, everyone," Elizabeth said. She was completely confused by this meeting, and it must have shown on her face because Clarissa stood up and met her at the door.

Clarissa was the epitome of shapeliness, and she looked as though she had stepped right out of a magazine.

"I can see the confusion on your face, so let me fill in the missing pieces."

Elizabeth was relieved and in awe at the same time. She gave herself a once over and thought she looked so underdressed next to Clarissa. Today she had on a blue sheath dress with pockets. She was going for casual, but now she felt frumpy. Clarissa had on a floral dress that moved with her and ended right above her knee. There was the same show of cleavage Elizabeth had seen at the town meeting, and Clarissa's hair was in that sloppy topknot that looked purposely messy.

"I'd appreciate it," Elizabeth said as she shook Clarissa's hand.

Clarissa showed her to the table for a seat. "Well, it turns out we heard you were engaged to Henry," she said.

Elizabeth plopped down in the seat and watched Clarissa clap her hands in joy before she took a seat at the table.

"How is that even possible?" Elizabeth asked. She looked at the three women who were on the opposite side of the rectangular table, looking at her with smiles.

"Well," Lydia said, "there was a gentleman, his name was Mr. Zecky; do you know him?"

Elizabeth nodded her head at the woman.

"Mr. Zecky came by the courthouse to check the name on the records. My office is in the courthouse. I do pro bono cases, and my husband Ethan, he works with me to help vet new businesses and offer opportunities to the Sweet Blooms community. He's absolutely amazing. You know he also—"

Clarissa interrupted her. "I have to stop her now; otherwise, she'll go on and on about Ethan. Not that he's not nice. Anyway, she's still in newlywed bliss where all her husband does is golden. What she was trying to say is Lydia is the free lawyer to those who can't afford, and the mayor's daughter, so Mr. Zecky spoke to her. I am on the council, and my office is also in the building. Any inquiries about land in Sweet Blooms I like to keep ahead of, so I was informed, and they were kind enough to bring Mr. Zecky to me. After talking to him, we realized that he was headed right by Daisy's place. So we had Mr. Zecky drop Daisy off as he was going to see you for some home check. We know how stressful relationships can be in Sweet Blooms and wanted to let you know that even though you are new here, you have someone you could talk to if need be."

"You look perfect for Henry," it was the last woman in the room and to Elizabeth, she looked like a flower child come to life. Her hair was long, she had what appeared to be a canvas bag around her shoulder and she was all smiles. Elizabeth couldn't remember seeing someone so happy.

Elizabeth didn't know what "perfect for Henry" was, but she was sure that wasn't something that could be applied to her.

"We completely understand why you're keeping it under wraps, but I want you to know that I don't think Hannah and Adam will mind at all."

Elizabeth nodded. She wasn't sure what she was nodding at, but it was just all so overwhelming that she couldn't even make a cohesive thought.

Clarissa reached out and touched her hand on the

table. "I know it seems like a lot, but we're here. I know you don't really know us, but we'd like to know you."

"Well, my main concern right now are my dogs and getting them settled," Elizabeth said.

Daisy nodded. "I know Henry. I know he will support you in whatever you do."

Elizabeth gave her a smile. "You seem to be very sure of Henry."

Daisy smiled. "He's been working on being a good neighbor."

Clarissa tapped her fingernails on the table, getting everyone's attention. Elizabeth looked at her and waited. She had a feeling that while Daisy and Lydia wanted nothing but the best for her, Clarissa was a little more everything. Clarissa was more confident, more bold and just more.

"So, Elizabeth, why don't you tell us how things are with you and Henry? I mean, we all heard his pitch at the council, but are you two okay?"

Elizabeth just couldn't believe she was in this situation. "Things aren't what I thought they would be."

"They rarely are, but I'm sure you two will find a way," Lydia chimed.

"What exactly is the problem? Money or Sex?"

"Neither!" Elizabeth replied quickly. "We don't have those types of problems. We are still just getting our communication together."

Daisy tsked. "I know what you mean. The men in Sweet Blooms can be a little stubborn."

Clarissa stood up and shrugged her shoulders. "Well, I'm not going to be of any help in the communication department. Now those other two problems? If you have any issues with those, give me a call. Ladies, I must be going. I have to go and spend Bain's money for a charitable cause."

Everyone waited until Clarissa left. When Elizabeth looked at the other two women, they had resigned looks on their faces.

"She's so Clarissa," Lydia groaned as she sat back in her chair. "Talking is not her forte."

"Making entrances and exits are," laughed Daisy. Daisy stood up.

"Well, Elizabeth, let me say that Henry is smart as a whip. He's made some mistakes, but he's a great neighbor and friend as well. I hope it goes well. I wanted to meet and greet you but I have to get back to the flower shop."

Now it was just her and Lydia in the room, and Elizabeth's head was still spinning.

"I want you to know we are here for you and also, we think you all make the most adorable couple ever with that sweet dog you brought with you."

Elizabeth smiled. "You're earning all sorts of brownie points with that comment."

"Well, at least we're doing that right. In case no one else has said it to you, welcome to Sweet Blooms.

"This is not the sexy look I see on television all the time with pets," Henry said, looking at Elizabeth pull the dog crates out of the minivan.

"Well, you can't believe what you see on television. At the end of the day, there is nothing sexy or delicate about transporting animals." Elizabeth had pulled out the dog crates and stood next to the closed crates breathing hard. "People don't realize loading and unloading crates is one of the more popular ways people hurt themselves. It causes back strain if you do it wrong or if you lift a crate that's too heavy."

"No fiber-light crates made just for women?"

"No. They're all durable for the animals and heavy." When Henry approached, she held out her hand to stop him.

"I think it's hard to look sexy and chic if you're panting and sweating."

Elizabeth looked at Henry and smiled. "You are so right. I had to tell the chic board that I couldn't be a member anymore." She knelt down to the kennel and opened the first crate, so Smiley could come out. The beagle waddled out cautiously, going into her lap.

"And you don't want me to help because?"

Elizabeth smiled. "It's not you. Smiley and Latte are older dogs. They know me, and I don't want them to be spooked. They've got work to do today."

Henry watched as she took the dogs out of their crates and put collars on them that had blinking lights. When Elizabeth had called and asked if it would be okay to survey the land, he had said yes.

She had explained that she was going to bring two dogs who would help her with the activity. He wasn't sure what activity the dogs were going to know better than him on his land, but he waited none-the-less. Now that they were here, he was beyond curious.

Elizabeth stood up, brushed off her dress and smiled. "You are looking a bit confused, Henry."

"I have to say when you said you wanted to survey the land, I thought we'd have to look at maps, but then you brought Smiley and what is the other one? That's a Dalmatian, right?"

Elizabeth smiled. "Yes, it is a Dalmatian. I'm sure the black spots on the all-white body gave it away."

Henry held up his hands. "Let's not be picky over why I know what it was. I want the brownie points that I knew what kind of dog it was."

"Fine, you have that. So I'll explain," Elizabeth said, as she walked the dogs towards an open area away from the house.

"There will be dogs on the property. We will try to make it as safe as possible, but a lot of the discovery and proofing of a property comes from the dogs themselves. Smiley and Latte, the Dalmatian, are going to wander, and I'll see if there are any obvious issues. The dogs are trained not to eat anything, but the little collars they have on record what they see and transmit it back to a server that I'll review later. This helps me survey the land from a dog's point of view."

"Okay, so what's next, you walk them, and you see what they see later via a recording?"

"Not quite," she said. Then Elizabeth bent down and unhooked them from their leashes. Smiley and Latte looked up at her for a moment and then began wandering.

Henry looked at both dogs going in opposite directions, and then he turned to Elizabeth.

"You're planning on getting them back how? Or was that why I was called, to corral senior dogs on the loose?"

Elizabeth laughed, and Henry stopped looking at where the dogs were going and looked at her. Even her laugh caught his attention and made him want to laugh with her. She had that rich laugh of a woman who didn't mind laughing out loud, it was the kind that invited others to laugh with her.

"No, I don't expect you to get the dogs." She put her hands about her neck and pulled out what looked to be a whistle.

"You have a dog whistle?" he asked. "Do they even work anymore?"

She looked at him as if he had lost his mind.

"What, you think all the cool dogs have iPhone apps that can listen for the dog whistle? Of course it still works." As if to prove it to him, she gave a short blow on the whistle, and moments later, Smiley and Latte bounded back into sight.

When she saw them she called out, "Good dog, go play."

Henry shrugged. "Okay, I can admit I'm wrong," Henry said. They went to sit on the bench in front of the house.

"You know how you said you could admit you were wrong. I'm going to have to do the same."

Henry cocked his head to the side. "Should I go get you some water or something stronger?"

Elizabeth laughed and shook her head. "I'm good. I don't need a drink. I just need to say this and move on."

"Okay, now I'm really interested."

"I received an invitation to chat at The Banter. I thought it was from you but when I got there, it was Lydia, Clarissa, and Daisy. They were all smiles. It seems they had met Mr. Zecky."

Henry gave her a look and then burst out laughing. When he had stopped himself from falling on the floor, he looked up to see that Elizabeth was not amused.

"Elizabeth, you don't have to apologize. I know Sweet Blooms. This is my home. I knew what I was signing up for when I decided to come back. I understand how news travels here."

She took a breath and blew it out. "When we spoke at Banter's, I thought you were crazy and paranoid. With the news going that fast, I can see how hard it must be not only to try to keep a secret but to keep everyone from knowing your business. My situation is an added stress that I never intended."

"Stress I can handle. The real question is going to be, can you handle it?"

"Well, I don't have as many options as you may think I do. I gave notice. I packed up my apartment and sunk all of my money into this project."

"You said you were in finance. I'm sure you could go back. Maybe stay with friends?"

"Are you trying to get rid of me, Henry?"

"No, I'm trying to make sure I give you a list of all of your options."

He looked at Elizabeth who had turn away and was looking towards the horizon. For a minute, he thought she had ended the conversation.

"I don't have friends, Henry. I once thought I did, but as it turns out, my friends were only there as long as I had money. In finance, failure is contagious, and there is no cure for it once you catch it."

Henry sat back in his seat and looked at her only to discover there was another depth to this amazing woman that had blindsided him again. From any other woman, he might have taken this confession as a sign that she wanted pity or empathy from him. Henry had been around women who made a living off of selling sob stories and getting a dime or two.

Elizabeth broke his rules on how he dealt with a woman. She rewrote the things he thought he knew, and she challenged him to rethink his old perceptions. Henry looked at her profile, proud and sure. She didn't bat her lashes for sympathy, and she didn't give the errant tear for compassion. This was Elizabeth. If she wanted something, she'd ask. She didn't play the games women who were unsure of their worth played. Henry found that because she owned up to what she did, he respected her. He found her appealing on every level and she made him think of what could be between them if he was looking for a relationship.

"Elizabeth what—"

She cut him off, stood up, and blew the whistle two times. The dogs came running around towards the house as if there was a race going on.

She turned towards him. "Thank you, Henry. I think the boys have been out enough. I'll have to get them back to the hotel and give them a good bath."

Henry nodded and she lit down the steps and went to gather the dogs into her car. She didn't look back, she didn't ask him for help loading them up, but she gave a last-minute wave to him as she drove away.

Henry stood on the wrap-around porch and let the evening breeze go through his hair. It was time to face facts. Elizabeth made him think about the future, made him think about tomorrow. She made him laugh. She made him remember not to be so serious. She awed him with her dedication to her cause even though he was sure she was wounded herself.

He shook his head. He couldn't believe he was even thinking about a woman who, for all essential purposes, came to take his land and ruin his reputation in town. He turned to go into the house. This was obviously a God-joke.

Seven

Elizabeth didn't know why she was nervous. She'd been to Henry's house several times. Although she hadn't been inside the house, she'd walked the grounds already, and her dogs had been here just two days ago, getting a feel for the place.

If the outside was any indication of what was going on inside, this visit would be an exercise in her biting her tongue. The front of the house had potential. She winced when she thought that word. She knew what it meant. It was code for, the house had good bones but needed a lot of work.

The house was a two-story home with a wraparound porch. The front yard, if that's what you wanted to call it, was decorated with patches of green. It wasn't sandy, but it was definitely bald in some places. With no fenced off front yard and cars having the ability to just drive up to the front, it didn't encourage grass growth.

When he had called her and asked if she could stop by, she knew he had come to a decision. They weren't due to meet again for another three days. It was glaringly obvious what this talk was about. Elizabeth dressed in a comfy dress with pockets. It was a rich green and made her feel confident and strong. She thought she might need all the help she could get.

When she arrived at the door, she didn't even have a chance to knock as it was yanked open before she even reached out her hand.

"Hello Elizabeth, thanks for stopping by," Henry said with a relieved smile.

As Elizabeth stepped into the house, she took her first look into his home.

"Well, I have to say Henry, I didn't really think this was an optional meeting."

He stood at the door and rubbed the back of his neck nervously.

"I guess you're right, but I didn't want you to feel forced. I wanted this to be—"

"What? Friendly? I'm not sure what you were thinking, but we both know why I'm here, and I'd like to get to it."

Henry cleared his throat and nodded. "I'm sure you would like for me to move through this, but this will affect both of our lives. So please come in and take a seat."

Elizabeth turned from Henry to take in her surroundings. She found herself standing in the most beautiful living room that she had ever seen. In front of her was a couch that was more of a rounded sectional with a pattern of fall leaves on it. In front of the couch was a coffee table and a large, circular green rug.

Then, as if it had been an afterthought, there were two chairs in the corner with a small table between them. The chairs looked more like recliners, and they exuded comfort. Elizabeth gave a moment contemplating sitting in the chairs versus the couch. If she was about to get her dreams taken from her, she wanted to look him in the face when he did it.

She went to the circular sofa and took a seat. She folded her hands in her lap and then waited.

"Well," he said, standing next to the sofa. "I want to thank you for coming.'

"You said that already," she replied.

She could see that he was fidgety and didn't seem to be able to sit down. If this was how he handled giving out bad news, it was no wonder that he'd left the business world.

"Do you want anything to drink?"

"Listen, Henry, I don't want anything except for you to get on with it." She wished he would speed this up. His antsiness was making her nervous.

He was dressed in jeans and a blue shirt rolled up at the elbows. She had to admit she liked the rolled-up sleeves look. It accentuated his arms. No matter what, he was still a fit man. A man who could garner the attention of any healthy woman. That would be, of course, if the woman was looking for a man.

"I want to tell you everything first. I wasn't upfront with Hannah, my ex, and I don't want to make that same mistake. It wasn't fair to her, and I promised myself I wouldn't do that to another person."

"Okay, what do you want to say?"

"Sweet Blooms' history," he said. He sat down and pulled her hands into his. "For as long as there has been a Sweet Blooms, there has been a Jenkins living on this land. You could almost say we're part of the founding fathers of the town."

"Solid roots." She watched him blink and then look down at their hands together. His thumb rubbed over her knuckles in a smooth way. The back and forth motion built up a warmth in her hand that took a life of its own and wove its way through her hand and up her arms.

"Roots that were rotten to the core," he whispered. "For as long as there have been Jenkins, there has been a womanizer and town drunk in Sweet Blooms."

Elizabeth felt his hands shake, and she gripped them within hers.

"Everyone expected me to mess up, and sure enough, I did. When I was growing up, there was a saying that if you dated a Jenkins, you had nowhere to go but up. I know you're doing this because you believe in what you're doing. But I would be living up to the Jenkins reputation if I didn't tell you. The town may treat you worse, or even pity you, if you tell them you are engaged to me."

"Well, the good news is I haven't gotten any pitying looks. I think Mr. Zecky took the long way around town, so there are already people who think it's true," she said with a slight smile. "They still let me into Banter's."

She saw him lift his head and look her in the eye. "I don't want you to ever know what it feels like to be shunned in public because of who you are, or because of me."

She pulled her hands out of his and cradled his face. "Look at me, Henry. I know when you see me, you see a well put together person, but I have a story. I was once homeless and had given up on life. If it hadn't been for Smiley, I might not be here today. I tell you this, so you'll know if it comes to that. I'm sure I can handle a couple of town gossips."

Henry smiled. "Says the woman who said no one would know."

Elizabeth smiled back and then pulled her hands to herself. "If we are going to do this, I want some ground rules between us."

"Like?"

"Like, you seem like a great guy, but this is just for the dogs. It's just until the grant gets done, and then we can break up any way you want and go our separate ways. I'm not looking to trap you or fall in love."

Henry looked at her and cocked his head to the side.

"What?" she asked.

"I'm not sure if I should be offended?"

Elizabeth shook her head. "No, it's not you Henry. I just don't have a lot of luck in love. I bring out the worst in everybody, and it never goes well."

A corner of his mouth turned up. "You have to see how funny this is. You don't want to fall in love because you're unlucky, and you said that with a straight face after I told you every man in my line is a wastrel."

Elizabeth returned the smile. "It just means we are evenly matched in our intentions."

Henry put his hand out for her to shake. Elizabeth grabbed it and gave him a firm shake.

"Well, Ms. Butler, it looks like you have yourself a fiancé."

Elizabeth reached over and hugged him. "You'll see this will be over before you know it."

She looked at him, smiling at her. His eyes were sable brown and bright. His lashes were long and curled the way any woman would envy. He wasn't like her ex, Lance. Lance had been predatory, and his smiles never made it to his eyes. There was no warmth in Lance's eyes like there was in Henry's.

She got up and made it to the door. Both of them were still smiling like fools.

Once she was out of the house and in her car, driving back to the hotel, it hit her. She had just willingly gotten into a loveless engagement again. Except this time she had her eyes wide open, and she wouldn't end up on the street with nothing but her name. She'd protect her heart and stick to the plan. Part of the plan was definitely, no falling in love. No good could come from it.

Eight

"I hope you're not really slow because I don't want to miss the March of the Penguins," Jerry said as he slid into the booth with Henry. Henry lifted his head up from his plate and swallowed the bite of his bacon cheeseburger with sweet potato fries.

"Jerry, I don't think you're in the right—"

"You're absolutely right. The reason I'm here is that you are not thinking."

Henry had known Jerry all his life. Jerry had been in Banter almost as much as his wife, Geeta. Normally, all of his interactions had been with Geeta, and Jerry just grunted. Everyone knew that Jerry had only one soft spot, and that was his family. For Geeta and Vihaan, he would move the world.

Knowing how outspoken Jerry could be about his opinion. Henry still didn't know what he had done to warrant this visit. Jerry had on blue jeans and a polo shirt, so he had clearly prepared for the meeting.

"So, let's get to it, son."

Henry put the burger down and sat back in the booth. "Jerry, you have me at a disadvantage."

"I sure do, and don't you forget it!"

"No, I mean, I don't know why you are here."

"I'm here because my Geeta has to go to celebrate the birthday of Gandhi with her sister. That means she has no time to work with you. So I had to come out."

Henry was stilled confused. It must have shown on his face.

"You came into Banter and ordered comfort food. Geeta has no time to comfort you today, so she sent me."

Henry wanted to laugh so bad the only thing he could do was look into his plate and wait for the urge to pass.

"Boy, you ain't foolin' no one looking down on that plate. In fact, it's because you have such poor performance that I'm here."

That got Henry to lift his head. "I appreciate whatever it is that Geeta wanted to do but—"

Jerry leaned forward over the table and beckoned Henry closer. He leaned over until his head touched Jerry's.

"Geeta said you have woman trouble," Jerry whispered.

Henry sat back as if Jerry had hit him. "Woman trouble? I don't have—"

Jerry sat back. "The word is you're engaged to the pretty gal who's going to be putting her dogs on your property."

"Yes she is, but that doesn't mean—"

"Taking care of pets together is almost like having kids for some. Are you two intending on playing house out there?"

"No, we aren't. It's not like that, Jerry."

"Really? Well, why don't you tell me what's it's like?

Where I'm sitting, two healthy kids are on one farm with a bunch of four-legged kids, and they are engaged. Did I miss something?"

Henry tried to think of what to say. "You know I'm a Jenkins."

"Yeah, boy, I know. I also know we make our future's, it's not given to us by our fathers."

Henry stopped, and at that moment, he was beyond grateful he knew Jerry. He hadn't known he needed to hear that. If he had been alone, it might have caused him to choke up, but he was with Jerry, and right now, he just wanted him to know he needed that support.

"Thanks, Jerry," Henry said in a low voice. "No one has bothered to say that to me before."

"Well, it needed saying. Was there anything else? You got a problem with the nice gal?"

"No, I don't, but it's not that way—"

"You don't find her beautiful? I mean, she's not my Geeta, but she's good for your age."

Henry laughed. "I find her very beautiful."

"Is she empty in the head?"

"No, she's really smart."

"Good, good. Are you having man problems, you know downstairs?"

Henry looked at Jerry as he jerked his head to the side to avoid looking him in the eye. Then it hit him what he meant.

"No, no, my plumbing is good."

"Well, the only thing left is money. Is she a money digger?"

Henry's lips turned up at the edges. "No, she's not a gold digger."

Jerry harrumphed. "I know the expression, boy. You

don't have enough money for her to be a gold digger anyway."

Henry looked at Jerry and let out a breath. "I'm not really engaged to Elizabeth. We're just pretending so she can get the grant proposal for her dogs." Henry waited for the backlash and the judgment; instead, he got a whole different response.

Jerry started laughing. He laughed so hard he needed to get some water from the table. Henry was confused.

"I don't think it's funny. It could be bad if others knew."

Jerry wiped his eyes. "So let me get this straight. You are pretending to be engaged."

"Yes."

Jerry picked up a napkin and wiped his mouth. "I'll tell Geeta you two are on your way."

"On our way?"

"Tell me how many other women will you give your name to in the town? Is it a habit or—"

"No, No," he said indignantly.

"Well, then half the work is already done. You young kids are a tad slow."

"Slow?"

Jerry stood up. "You really need to get that habit you have of repeating whatever it is that you hear. If you do that enough times, some people will think you have a problem."

"Did you hear what I said?"

Jerry yawned. "Boy the question isn't did I hear what you said, but did you hear what you said? You kids today are quick on the tech but slow on the thinking."

"What are we talking about?"

"Well, now that we've had this talk, we're not talking about a thing. I'll tell Geeta you're going to be just find and fumble through things like kids do."

"Jerry, can you explain?"

Jerry looked at his watch. "Actually, I can't. I have to get back to see the march. You'll get it. You might go the long way, but you'll get it."

Henry watched Jerry leave. While it wasn't clear what he was doing with Elizabeth, it was clear to him that he needed to take responsibility about being engaged a little more seriously if this was going to be pulled off.

He knew just what to do for his fiancé this evening.

Elizabeth thought once the decision was made, she could forget about it. It became very obvious very quickly that this was not the sentiment of Sweet Blooms. When she was leaving the hotel the next morning to take Latte and Smiley out, the front desk clerk made sure to tell her where the bridal store was in town and that she had a cousin who could knit and/or sew wedding garments for dogs of all sizes. The contact information would be on her bed when she came back. Elizabeth didn't know which one was more distressing, that she was offering advice for the event or that the contact information would be in her room on her bed and not in a message somewhere outside of her room.

She had several places to stop today. She wanted to make sure she made it to the local kennel and she hoped she'd be able to get to the general store. She was told in the community center there was a store where you could buy some goods that were made in the classes.

Elizabeth had been running errands for most of the day. Every time she stopped somewhere, she would get a handshake that lasted a bit too long with a friendly phrase of welcome. If they weren't shaking her hand, they had suggestions of where to go for bridal advice. One or two people even suggested a decorator because the Jenkins men weren't known for their decorating taste.

Elizabeth was fed up with everyone and their helpful tips and tools for a newly engaged woman. When she got a message from Henry to meet him at his place, she was more than ready to tell someone what she thought about small towns and the lack of privacy. When she arrived at his place, she found him in jeans and a blue t-shirt. She could see a fine sheen of sweat on his forehead and a bright-eyed alertness that always seemed to be with him.

"One, stop looking so happy in this hot weather, and two, how can it be that everyone in this town knows we are engaged?" she ratted out breathlessly. After the words were out of her mouth, she contemplated if she should have been so aggressive towards the man that was helping her reach her dream.

Henry wasn't fazed. Instead of rising to the challenge in her voice, he held out his arms and smiled. "Small towns, aren't they amazing?"

"There is no privacy, and people who didn't even know I existed said hello to me and offered advice on my upcoming marriage. They didn't even care about the engagement, or when I corrected them and said we're just engaged, they smiled at me like I was a slow person or something."

"We don't really do engagements in Sweet Blooms."

"What? Do you think you could have mentioned it before?"

Henry shrugged his shoulders and then had a very thoughtful look on his face.

"You know Elizabeth, now that I've thought about it, the only time you really hear about someone being engaged, it is usually a sign that they don't have enough money to marry right away."

After hearing that statement, Elizabeth stopped and looked at Henry.

"Tell me, oh great one, did it occur to you at any time to let me know about the secret language of engagements in Sweet Blooms?"

"Ever live with something for so long you don't think about it anymore? That would be one of those things. Now that I'm thinking about it, I'm going to have to do something about that," he said as he turned and walked towards the barn.

She was confused and lost about what he meant. She didn't like not knowing, and at this point, she felt as though there was a lot she didn't know. At any other time, Elizabeth might have left and gone home, but this time she followed him. She was going to have to work this out with Henry. She needed to be back in control, and they needed a plan.

As she followed him to the barn, she could feel a tingle running through her body. If she really looked at it, she might call it excitement. It had been a while since she'd had the banter that went on between men and women. She wasn't sure she was any good at it.

That was assuming she was ever good at it.

She watched him in front of her. He had a slow, easy

gait. The man looked good coming and going. It wasn't like she was really interested in him in that way, but Elizabeth couldn't help but look where she was going, right? The sight of lean legs, sure strides, and a pleasing view was just coincidental.

When she walked into the barn, he was standing in the middle of it. He stood, legs shoulder-width apart, and looking at Elizabeth in a way that made her run her hands through her hair and smooth some non-existent wrinkles from the side of her dress.

"Come closer, Elizabeth."

The words came out in a slow, easy way that seemed to seep into her bones and loosen her up. Henry looked like he was braced for something. She couldn't just stand by the barn gate so she looked in the barn. Nothing looked different. The two horses were in the stall, looking on as if to bear witness to what was about to happen.

Elizabeth took a step closer.

The edge of his mouth tipped up as he looked at the step she took. Rolling her eyes, she crossed her arms over her chest and started to walk towards him. Who did he think he was? Her fiancée or something? This was all make-believe, fake. So why did it feel so real?

"What's the big deal about how close I am?"

He didn't say anything. He just looked at the spot in front of him and waited. She practically dragged her feet to get there. When she was in the spot he had requested, she was close enough to see the amused grin on his face.

He leaned down, and she could feel his breath against her ear. When he spoke, it was a soft stream of warm air against her neck.

"You don't like taking instructions, do you?"

"Nonsense, I don't mind doing things that make sense."

"Ahh, so that's how you get around it."

She turned her head towards that teasing voice and stopped when she realized how close she was to him. Her eyes glanced upwards, but his mouth captivated her. Were men supposed to have attractive lips? His lips were bracketed by dimple marks that spoke of someone who knew how to laugh.

So here she was next to Mr. Sexy himself, and her tongue nervously went over her bottom lip. Had she forgotten her lip-gloss? Could she put some on before he noticed? He was looking like he just stepped out of the tropical commercials, and her skin looked like one of the lizards running on the grounds.

She cleared her throat, hoping to clear her head at the same time. "I'm not trying to get around anything."

He took a step back and smiled. "In the first stall is Red."

Elizabeth looked at the brown horse and then at Henry. "Whoever named that horse Red, is color blind."

He went towards the horse, who pawed the ground while watching him carefully. "The reason she's called Red isn't because of her coloring; it's because of her temperament."

She watched him approach the mare slowly and then reach out a hand palm up again. He didn't shove his hand into her face or rush to touch her in any way. He waited. When the mare had settled down and appeared ready, he laid his hand on her nose.

Elizabeth watched him. She wouldn't have thought that he had the patience to woo a horse, but he did.

With everything else going on, she didn't need to see this part of him.

He turned towards her and held out his hand. "Let's try this again, Elizabeth. I want to make sure this goes well for the both of us."

She looked at his hand suspiciously, but she took it.

"Elizabeth, there are rules to being engaged in a small town."

She looked at him and tried not to grit her teeth. "How come you didn't decide to tell me about the rules until now?"

Henry gave her a small smile. "I wouldn't think to tell you something that I thought was common knowledge, Beth."

"Are you putting this on me? And who told you, you could call me Beth?"

Henry smiled, reached out and twisted a lock of her hair around his finger.

"Don't you think it's going to be odd, me calling you Elizabeth, when we're planning on getting married? Engaged couples have nicknames for each other. Would you like something more endearing like Buttercup or maybe Sweetie Pie or—"

Holding her hand up she said, "Just stop! There will be no butter-nothing, or sweetie-whatevers. You may call me Beth."

His voice was gentle, and it wrapped around her and soothed the nervousness that had been her constant companion. She could hear the twirling of her hair, and it was comforting in its own way.

She should have thought of it earlier, that if they were engaged, they should have some kind of relationship, right? She could do this. It's true she wasn't in a relationship, but that was because she didn't want to be in one, not because she couldn't.

She looked at Henry and took a deep breath. He was just a man. She could do this.

It was as if he could tell what she was thinking. He stepped a little closer to her and said in a loving voice, "Hello, Beth."

Elizabeth rolled her eyes. "Whatever."

"That doesn't sound very loving to me."

She closed her eyes and tried to gather herself. His subtle tones vibrated in the air and then wrapped themselves around her.

She opened her eyes and gave him her best smile. "I'm sorry, dear. Of course, you can call me Beth."

"You need to say that with less of a dagger look in your eye," he chuckled.

She knew she was making this harder than it had to be, but Henry wasn't what she had been expecting. "Okay, we've made nice, now let's move on."

"Hold on, Beth. If you think the pet names are all there is to a relationship, then we may have a real problem."

"What else are you looking for?"

He let the curl that he had been twisting, and her hair fell against her cheek. It was still warm from his touch, and she leaned into it.

"I want you to be comfortable, Beth. What else are you willing to give?"

His calling her Beth sent waves of anticipation through her. Who knew what a name could do.

"Henry, don't make this difficult. Just tell me what it is you want me to do. What are these rules?"

Henry reached out and tucked the strand of hair behind her ear.

"First, everyone will assume we know something about each other's family."

Elizabeth shrugged. "I don't have any. I'm alone."

He stopped moving and then trailed his hand down her cheek until it was under her chin, and then he lifted her head so that he was looking directly into her eyes.

"I've got a brother, but he doesn't come around. He hasn't spoken to me since my son's birth when he told me he was disappointed in me that I was turning out to be just like our dad. So, for all intents and purposes, I'm alone too."

How did he do that? Elizabeth wasn't sure if she should run into his arms or cry for them both. Again, it was as if he could read her mind.

"Don't feel bad for me, Beth. I've actually made out way better than I've deserved. I met Hannah, who is amazing. We had an even more amazing son. Hannah and Nathan have a stable life. I've got a little bit of coin in my pocket now that I can share with Hannah for the times when I wasn't there. Nothing makes up for the missed time, but I'll do what I can do now. The best thing about it all is I've got you, even if it's only for a short time."

"Okay, no feeling bad for Henry. Check. What else are we supposed to do? We know each other's families. We have pet names. Anything else on the checklist of engagement?"

"There are two more things we have to cover, and then we'll be done."

"Good, what are they? We have to do the genetic test in one of those mail-away kits?"

"No, but we have to say that there is at least one thing we really like about the other person."

"Okay, you go first so I can understand how this works?" she said it as a challenge because she wasn't sure if he wasn't just fishing for compliments from her.

He didn't hesitate. "You care deeply enough to follow your passions. You take risks for things you love, and you're honest."

She stepped away from him.

"You think you know a whole lot about me, don't you?" she said in a small voice.

Henry shrugged. "It's not just me. Other people see that in you as well."

"So, I'm popular discussion in the café or at Banters? I mean, I've heard it's hard to get on the gossip plate in either one of those places."

Henry smiled. "I'm not saying you're top billing or anything, but I'll say that you do make it up there pretty high. Listen, I'm not the best pick when it comes to a lot of things, but I'll get you through this. Now it's your turn, try to think of something you like about me, or something that you want me to tell you about myself."

Elizabeth was standing in his shadow. She was close enough to touch him, but far enough to see him clearly. This had seemed so easy when she first drove here. He wanted to know what she liked about him. It was turning out that there wasn't a whole lot not to like about him. He admitted his mistakes. He knew what he had done. He didn't make excuses. What did she like about him? What didn't she like about him? How had she gotten here? Was it even possible she might have feelings for the man she thought was the safest person to be around?

Henry cleared his throat. "I knew it would be hard for you to come up with something, but I didn't think it would be this hard."

"No, no, it's not you. I think I like you, Henry. Like a person or something?"

Henry chuckled. "I guess that's good. Liking me as a person is good. I mean, you could like me like a dog. No, I can't say that because I might be in better shape if you liked me the way that you like your dogs."

Elizabeth laughed. "Okay, enough with that. So I like you as a person, and I think you're upfront and not bad to look at."

Henry closed the distance between them. He picked up her hands and held them in his. "You're trembling."

"It's cold out here," she lied. "Fall is near."

She wanted to say that this situation officially scared the heck out of her. She wanted to take back the words she'd already said about him. Elizabeth wished for something to happen that would take his attention off of her.

"You said two things, right?"

He looked into her eyes and tucked her hair back behind both of her ears. "You've got a good memory; the second one is this."

Before she could say a thing, he leaned down and placed a light kiss on her lips.

It had been a while since she'd been kissed. After Lance's betrayal, she was relationship shy. Even so, this kiss was different than Lance's. When Lance kissed her, she had to make sure she had her hand on her wallet.

This kiss was from a man that she knew really liked her. It raised feelings she shouldn't have had. It made her question where she stood and look at her goals. It made her look at Henry like a man and not a partner in her business.

The kiss wasn't an exploratory kiss. In fact, she'd have to say it was pretty chaste. But she wasn't expecting it.

He lifted his head and looked down at her. "Are we okay?"

She looked at him and nodded. "We're okay."

She would have said more, but the honking of a car broke the mood. They broke apart.

"We'd better go," Henry said as he gave her time to pull herself together.

When they did exit the barn, they stopped and looked out in shock as they saw an orange convertible with the door open and a man calling out, "Elizabeth!"

Henry looked over at her. "A friend of yours?"

She looked at him. "In case I kill him before you two are introduced, that's Lance."

"Your ex?"

"That's him."

Nine

"Elizabeth!"

Elizabeth shook her head at the sound of her name on Lance's lips. Why did he always elongate her name so it sounded more like E-lee-zaa-beth.

"What do you want, Lance? I don't have any money or connections you'd want."

"Elizabeth, don't be crass. At least greet me as if we have some history together."

Lance Classon waited by his car for Elizabeth to come to him. Elizabeth took her sweet time. She remembered once upon a time she was so enamored with his looks. Lance was five foot eleven with dark, lush hair, and a gym-body that looked good in suits as well as workout clothes.

Today was no exception. Lance was dressed in a blue striped shirt rolled up to the elbows and a white polo shirt beneath, and faded blue jeans. All of it made him look like a model, or at the very least a ken doll.

Lance was in his early forties, but he could compete for looks with a man in his late twenties. Elizabeth remembered how she had thought Lance was the smartest person ever. Now she knew he was probably the most ruthless person she had ever met.

She remembered how she had once looked upon him with the eyes of innocence and love. She thought that his drive and dedication had been a sign of his concentration on trying to help others. She had been wrong.

Lance was dedicated. He was dedicated to making money and getting ahead.

As she got closer to Lance, she could feel her chest starting to feel tighter. He had been all of her dreams in one person. He had been the knight in shining armor who would always be there. Instead, he had turned out to be an illusion.

Lance pushed himself off of his car and smiled at her. "You look very native, Elizabeth."

"Not that it's your business, but this is my preferred way of dressing." Elizabeth stopped in front of Lance and crossed her arms over her chest. She looked at him and wondered how she could have missed how shallow and self-serving he was. "What do you want?"

"So much for old times."

"You don't believe in old times. You hold only with the dollar. So I have to ask you again. Why are you here?"

Lance looked around the yard and then back at her. "You're not even going to invite me into the house?"

Elizabeth didn't bother to look over her shoulder.

"No, I don't want to dirty the house. Again, what do you want here?"

"Did you ask the man behind you what he was doing here?" Lance asked, pointing towards Henry. It wasn't until that moment that she remembered that Henry was here.

"I didn't ask him because it's his place. Don't tell me you didn't know that."

Lance shrugged. "I thought he'd left the property."

Henry cleared his throat. "He has not left the property, but he has work to do in the barn. Beth, let me know when you're done."

Men! Elizabeth couldn't believe he had decided to use the pet name right now. She could see Lances' eyebrows lift, and his eyes squint to get a better look at Henry. This was so not what she needed in her life right now.

Lance stared after Henry for a few more moments before turning to Elizabeth. She was waiting for the Lance she knew to come out. He looked at the two cars in the driveway and then back at her.

"I know you know how to make money Elizabeth. Why are you driving that small car? Does it even have air conditioning?"

Elizabeth looked at her car and Henry's truck. She knew Lance saw cheap, low-quality vehicles. At best, they could carry things to and fro. He'd never be caught in a transport vehicle, and both of the cars would qualify. "Yes, it does have air conditioning, not that I need it. I know how to drive with the windows down."

Lance looked at her as if she had lost her mind. Elizabeth would have thought it was funny if it weren't for the fact that she knew he was serious.

"Is this how far you've fallen? You can't afford the basics?"

Elizabeth laughed. "A year ago, I was homeless. A car that I can pay for makes me feel like a rich person."

Lance's eyes widened, and then he crossed his arms over his chest. "You are so dramatic, Elizabeth. Did you think I would believe you were homeless? I mean, I know you lost everything, but there's always a backup account Elizabeth, every good finance person knows this. But that's in the past. Why doesn't he call you by your proper name?"

"It's Beth to him."

"Beth? It's like some rural woman's name. You're missing the second part. Like Beth Ann. It's not a grown woman's name," he chided.

"Well, if a grown woman's name is what you called me, I'll take Beth, thank you." Had she really seen something in him? Her taste was beyond bad if this was the type of man she was attracted to. When she looked at Lance, she had to also ask the question if this was still the kind of man that she was attracted to. Was Henry just the country version of Lance?

"Well, I can see that you are just as stubborn as ever," Lance said with a disapproving tone.

Was she stubborn? She had to fight off the sudden insecurity that always seemed to come when Lance spoke. He always sounded so sure of what he was saying.

"I can't imagine you came here, Lance, just to remind me that I'm not up to snuff," Elizabeth said. "Can you get to the point and let me know why you're here?"

Lance pushed away from the car and walked up to her. "I was the one who referred Mr. Zecky to you."

"You did, and I thanked you. I had to do the rest of the work to get the grant done," Elizabeth said. She put her hand over her mouth. "Oops, did I say that with my outside voice?" she said sarcastically.

"You know the way it works. I help you, and you help me."

Elizabeth looked at him, and the feeling that she was

missing something was starting to bring her a constant state of unease.

"Why are you here?"

"I'm here to make sure everything goes well. I'm here for you."

Elizabeth gave him a sideways look. "Really? You left me when I lost my job. You wouldn't answer my calls when I told you I had nowhere to go, and when I finally caught up with you outside of your co-op, you had the police take me away as a vagrant. You can understand how I might not believe a word you say now."

Lance smiled. "It was a misunderstanding. You know that when people are on the downslope, anyone they touch, can be taken with them."

"You could have helped me, Lance."

Lance exhaled. "If I had helped you, it would have been an ongoing cycle. Help you once. Help you twice. It would have gone on and on. You wouldn't be here if I had interfered before." He spread out his hands and shook his head. "I thought you would be more grateful for all I've done for you."

Elizabeth looked at Lance and wondered if he really believed what he was saying. "I'm obviously not at a point in my life that I can appreciate all you've done for me."

Lance nodded and then turned toward the sports car. "I can see you're right. I think we need some space for you to think about what I've said. I'll be in town for a bit, and then we can go over business."

Elizabeth watched him get into his car and she was torn between telling him to go away and never come back, or to force him to tell her why he really came.

As he drove away, she thought about the day and decided she needed some space. She knew Henry would back her up, but she needed to think, and she couldn't do that here.

<h1 style="text-align:center">Ten</h1>

"What can I get you?" the woman asked behind the Sweet Blooms Cafe bar. "I can see a pretty girl like you is here alone, so you're not feeling your best. Is there anything you're allergic to?"

Elizabeth looked up at the kind woman and smiled. After leaving Henry's place, she drove to her hotel and decided she didn't want to be alone. She saw Sweet Blooms Café and decided to numb her pain with the confectionary delights everyone touted existed here.

"I've got no allergies," Elizabeth said.

Elizabeth thought the older woman was sweet, but she wasn't ready to let her pick the days special for her. Instead, she picked up the menu on the counter and gave it a once over. She had already decided on the carrot cake. It was not too sweet with a hint of healthy to it. She got ready to give her order when the woman on the other side of the bar held up her hand.

"Let me guess. You want a carrot cake?"

Elizabeth just nodded. The woman smiled and patted the bun on top of her head.

"Well, it's nice to know I still have my touch. My name is Rose, by the way. I don't work here often, but sometimes my son and daughter-in-law need a hand and I help out. You stay right there, and I'll get them to get you a slice of cake."

She watched the woman as she left and turned around to stare at the crowd in the store. She could definitely see the appeal. It was designed like an old ice cream shop with black and white tiles on the floor. Elizabeth was sure you could gain weight just from sniffing the air. There were two-seaters for couples, booths for family or a large group of friends, and the back opened up to the back yard. Yes, she could see why so many came.

Today she was one of the many and obviously she was as transparent as Lance always accused her of being. Certainly she had learned something from her last encounter with Lance.

Elizabeth was brought out of her thoughts by the humming of the woman behind the counter. What was her name? Yes, Elizabeth remembered, it was Rose.

"Thank you, Rose," Elizabeth said as Rose put the plate of carrot cake in front of her.

"I'm glad you remembered my name; it will make everything else easier."

Elizabeth looked at her, and her confusion must have shown on her face.

Rose wiped her hands on her apron.

"What I'm trying to say is do you want to talk about your problem before or after you eat the cake? I mean the cake isn't going to get cold or anything. It's already cold," Rose laughed.

Elizabeth looked at the carrot cake and then at the woman.

"Do I look like I have a problem?" Elizabeth asked.

Rose waved her hand. "Now, don't go looking all pathetic. It's not that you have a sign on you that says, I've got issues. Well, not to everyone, at least. You need a little age and experience to see it."

Elizabeth looked at the woman and let out a sigh.

"Great, only 25% of the town will know that I've got a problem. In Sweet Blooms, that just means I've got two hours before everyone knows." With that proclamation, she dug into the carrot cake.

"You kids. As soon as there's any issue at all, you start to roll up in a ball and swear the world is coming to an end. You want help or not?"

Elizabeth shoved another piece of cake in her mouth. She couldn't remember the last time anyone had asked that question. Did she want any help? Well of course she wanted help, but she didn't want to discover she was just as naïve as she had been three years ago.

"Yes, I want to do better. It's why I came to Sweet Blooms. It's why I started over." Elizabeth looked at Rose, who was leaning on the counter watching her.

"Are you done?"

Elizabeth exhaled.

"Yes, I'm done," Elizabeth mumbled.

"Alright I'll help you, but I can't stand here all day, so we're going to have to take some short cuts. You know my body isn't what it used to be."

Elizabeth looked behind the bar. "Did you want me to get you a chair?"

She saw Rose look up at her and smile. "I said I was getting tired, not dead! Besides, I have to set you right first."

"Okay?"

"So, you came in here looking worse than a puppy left on the side of the road."

Elizabeth wanted to protest, but the fact of the matter was she probably did look pretty bad. "I did."

"Money, Man, or a child?"

Elizabeth cocked her head to the side and gave a small smile. "Are those my options?"

"Well, it turns out that you're young. You walked in here on your own two feet, and you didn't hesitate to order something sweet. I figure that makes your health okay. You didn't mind dropping money for the cake. And let me tell you I know those cakes aren't cheap. So I'm going to rule out money. That leaves old faithful, man."

Elizabeth chuckled. "You're pretty good at this."

"Let's just say I've got a kid or two, and some of them are daughters. So what is the problem?"

Elizabeth gave it some thought. "Don't you know who I am? I mean, I think most of Sweet Blooms knows who I am."

Rose turned around and made herself a cup of tea in a delicate blue and white mug that had a dainty floral print on it. She took a sip and then placed the cup on the counter.

"Child, listen to me. It's not about who I say you are. It's always about who you say you are. So have I heard the gossip on who you are? Yes, but I'm still waiting to hear what *you* say."

Elizabeth thought about that for a moment. Did she know who she was anymore?

"Whew, you're going to take a little longer than I thought! I'm getting old just waiting for you to come to a decision. Let's try something else. What made you doubt you knew what you were doing?"

Elizabeth nodded at that and took a deep breath. "My ex showed up in town. I know he's not here for anything good."

"Do you still love him?"

"No!"

"Then what's the problem?"

"Well, the problem is, he's here."

Ross set her cup down. "Are you about to tell me what my grandkids say? He's looking at me?"

Elizabeth felt indignant. "No, I'm not. It's just you don't understand Lance. He's sneaky and ruthless."

"If you know all this, then what is the problem?"

"When he comes around, everything is ruined. I was with him before, and it went south and—and—"

Rose reached out her hand and placed it on top of Elizabeth's.

"And you don't want to be hurt by him anymore."

Elizabeth looked at the aged hand on top of hers. She let Rose's words sink in. It was true, she didn't want to be hurt anymore.

She could still remember when she first met Lance. She had her first job in an accounting firm, and she met Lance in a meet-and-greet. When she saw him, he appeared polished, knowledgeable, and handsome. She was lost from their first meeting.

Three months later, they had become an item. She hadn't moved in with him, but she stayed with him almost every day. Then he had told her about a good deal that he couldn't invest in, but he wanted her to make a profit from. She had invested in it, and under Lance's guidance, she'd put everything in. He had made a profit for suggesting her, but the deal had gone bad.

In finance, when things go bad, nothing is sacred from recoupment. The deal went south, and all of her possessions and money were confiscated, garnished, or put on hold. She tried to reach out to Lance, but he wouldn't return her calls. She was barred from the co-op.

The humiliation and decimation of her life was done quickly. Within a week, she lost her home, money, and friends. She wound up living on the street. She was depressed and lost. Elizabeth was sitting on a street corner wallowing in how bad her life was when Smiley limped up next to her. He crawled into her lap and then looked up to kiss her on the nose. At that moment, Smiley saved her life.

With Lance showing up again, he reminded her that she didn't want the despair of knowing she was alone or that someone who had cared for her had betrayed her. Elizabeth didn't know if she could go through that again.

Rose tapped her hands, and Elizabeth looked up to see her smiling. Elizabeth could feel the heat of tears coming, and she tried to blink them back.

"Child, don't cry, fight. You are a better, wiser woman. Hold on to the woman you've become. You'll find that he may throw a loop after you, but you'll be able to fend it off this time. Besides, if the town gossip is true, you're engaged to the Jenkins boy."

Elizabeth cleared her throat. Henry. Just thinking about Henry made her giddy and scared all at the same time. She heard the rap of a wooden spoon on the counter.

Rose waved that wooden spoon at her.

"Don't you even start going down the path of wondering if all men are alike. If they were, no woman would marry them. Now I can't speak to your other fellow. Maybe it was a time that you were just young and dumb. I find the younger generation will pick something flashy before they find out if there's anything behind it. Now that Henry boy? He's made some mistakes. I know his stock isn't all that good either. I think he was going down the wrong path, but he pulled himself up, and now I think he's doing the right thing."

Elizabeth smiled as she watched Rose put the wooden spoon down with one hand and picked up her teacup with the other.

"Do you think Henry is okay? You don't think you might be a little biased since he's from here?"

Rose waved her statement off. "Child, time can be short, and I have no time to be beating around the bush. Whether he's was from here or not, I'd tell you. You know we women got to stick together."

Elizabeth pushed the carrot cake to the side. "Thank you, Rose."

Rose gave her a big smile and then rubbed her hip.

"Child, you didn't need to know—what do the young kids say? The skinny?—on your ex. You just wanted to make sure you weren't alone. As for Henry, my words will bear out. Now, if you'll excuse me. I'll send someone to finish up. Good day Elizabeth and remember, you're a part of Sweet Blooms now."

<h1 style="text-align:center">Eleven</h1>

"Anal sacs have to be cleaned," Elizabeth said to the group. "When strays come in, this will be a part of their monthly maintenance, so let's not be squeamish, and let's get it done."

She looked at the two teen volunteers that had signed up to work at the ranch. They had their terriers on the table with their gloved hands and proud smiles. With the coming of Sweet Inspirations, Elizabeth knew she needed some volunteers to help out. Until the money actually came, she wasn't sure she could offer any money. Grooming strays, assessing their health, clipping nails, and expressing anal sacs were all part of the job.

Henry had given her temporary use of the barn. There she could set up some crates for about five dogs in the stalls next to the horses. He also gave her a long wooden worktable that was waist-high. It was just the right height to set the dogs on to help train the volunteers. It was a great staging area for her and the trainees that came in.

After giving the teens a thumbs-up, she walked down the table to see the two women who had joined.

Every now and again, Henry would come into the barn to take the horses out to pasture or do some grooming on them himself. The two women each had a small terrier in front of them, but each time Elizabeth looked over at the table, she saw the women craning their necks to look at Henry.

She guessed she should have suspected that some of the local women would come by to see the "engagement," but this was a bit much. The flyer had told them they would get dirty, but these women were in floral sundresses and fashionable sandals. When he walked by, he nodded, but to his credit, he didn't pay the women any more attention than he did the teens.

Elizabeth stood in the view of the two women.

"Hello, Ladies, I want to thank you for volunteering. I notice those sacs aren't cleaned up, is there a problem?"

The shortest of the two women, a curvy brunette, looked at Elizabeth. "I think the teens should be doing this, and we could do something else more fitting to us."

Elizabeth expected some excuse, and she wasn't disappointed. She tried to put on her best *I hear you, but we are still going to do it my way* smile.

"I could tell just from looking at you two that you were capable women. In animal rescue, women have to work harder and do more because of the belief that women will balk at having to do activities that are less than pleasant or potentially dangerous. Can you believe that?"

The women nodded but still had the confused look on their faces.

"However, I want you to know I don't believe in those silly rumors. I know women who have seven to nine children. They feed them, educate them, and take them to the park all by their lonesome. So I know every woman is able to do rescue work."

She leaned over the table and gently stroked the grey terrier that was looking up at her. Then she focused on the brunette with a stillness that only prey saw before they were consumed.

"I suggest you make a decision. You decide you want to help the strays or not. A dog can rub himself raw, get an infection, and die if their anal sacs aren't attended. I don't want to have to bury innocent animals that come to me for refuge because you thought the activity was beneath you."

When Elizabeth finished talking, she realized that the teens were watching them, as well as Henry. She focused on the brunette, whose lips were compressed, and disdain was in her voice when she spoke.

"You two deserve each other."

"You know that statement was probably the most productive thing you've done all day. Maybe rescue work isn't right for you."

"This kind of work isn't right for any reputable woman."

The second woman looked over her shoulder, sniffed at Elizabeth, and then followed the brunette out.

Elizabeth looked at the teens and Henry. She went to the teens' dogs, inspected them, and then picked them up in her arms.

"I want to make sure you've got it so you two can do those dogs there, and I'll be back," she said. The teens went to the dogs, and Henry nodded. After another hour and a half of toenail clipping and inspecting ears for mites and wax and then Elizabeth ended the class.

"Hey guys, I want to thank you for the work you put in today. The next session we do will be bathing, so bring a spare shirt."

The teens laughed and nodded. They'd be back. She put the last two dogs in their crates and made sure they were settled and okay. The rest of her dogs had been transported to a nearby shelter. The shelter couldn't hold them indefinitely, but it would do for now.

When she stood up, Henry was standing next to the table, looking at her.

"I've been waiting for my turn," he said with a smile.

"And exactly what were you waiting for?" Elizabeth asked as she cleared the table. She tried not to notice how he looked with the sun behind him. He was right off the cover of every cowboy romance she had ever read. Today he had on a short-sleeved shirt that showed off his muscled arms and trim waist. The only thing she could think of was that short sleeve shirt was one of the luckiest items to be hugging Henry close like that all day long.

"I wasn't sure if I would have to step in with your volunteers."

She stopped clearing the table and looked at him. "Were those friends of yours?"

Henry shrugged. "They introduced themselves as available if I needed to talk to someone who was from Sweet Blooms."

Elizabeth wasn't sure how things worked in Sweet Blooms, but she was sure about how she wanted her relationship to run. Even if the relationship wasn't real.

"Did you happen to take either one of them up on their standing offer for conversation?"

"Would it have mattered if I did?"

Elizabeth shook her head. "No, you're a free agent, but I'd hope that you would be discreet," she said.

"There's no need to be discreet. Everyone knows the truth."

Elizabeth stopped and crossed her hands over her chest. "If you didn't want to do this or if you already were with someone else, you should have told me. I mean was it one of the women who came because that's going to be really awkward to fix and—"

While she had been talking, Henry had made his way closer to her. He was standing next to her, and she was at a loss for words.

"You need to stop talking before I begin to believe that I might be involved with someone besides you."

Elizabeth looked up at him, and she could feel her mouth forming an Q. Then she covered her mouth with her hands. He pulled her hands away from her face.

"Have you taken any leadership or management classes?"

"Management classes? Not really, I mean, when I opened the fund I had to take basic classes to run the rescue. I feel pretty competent in knowing what needs to be done."

He reached up and tucked a strand behind her ear. "Maybe I could teach you a thing or two about giving and receiving orders."

Elizabeth tried to look anywhere except at his mouth. Elizabeth already knew he had two lips that were perfectly shaped as if Michelangelo himself had carved them.

"Do you think I'm doing something wrong?" Elizabeth asked. "Are you thinking that you shouldn't agree with signing the papers or that you want to reach out to Mr. Zecky because you think I'm not fit and that maybe you are more fit than I am?"

"I'm not questioning your judgment or my role in signing the papers."

"Then I don't understand?"

Henry smiled. "I thought the talk of management and giving orders might go another way. Maybe with you wanting to give me orders or—"

Elizabeth shook her head and put her hand on Henry's chest.

"Hold up. Are you trying to tell me you were trying to do some flirting with me?"

"Yes."

Elizabeth laughed. "Oops! I mean, I didn't mean to laugh out loud, but I don't think that, well, what I'm trying to say is I wouldn't have thought that was a way to go. I'm just not that kind of girl. You know the giggle thing and the flirty thing. I've never mastered the art."

Henry stepped back, and Elizabeth could see he was confused.

"Henry I'm not sure why you thought flirting was necessary."

"We're engaged Beth, we're supposed to play. Or at the very least look like we play with each other often."

"Let's try it again. It looks like both of us might be out of practice," she said with a smile.

"Okay but—"

"Shhh, I've had management classes, so I know how to plan things," she said with a smile. Henry grinned and nodded.

"Thank you for not going out with the women while we are together."

"Why would I even think of it when I'm with you?" Henry asked.

Elizabeth looked up at him and swallowed. "Thanks."

"There's nothing to thank me for. I'm engaged to a woman who is beautiful and compassionate. Why would I look anywhere else? I'm happy with the way things are now."

Elizabeth let out a breath and could feel her throat going dry. She cleared her throat and then gave him a smile.

"Henry I—"

He closed the distance between them and placed two fingers on her lips.

"I admit I blew it at first, but this time I need you to accept this compliment. How we got here doesn't matter as much as the fact that we are here in the moment, and I couldn't think of a better person I'd like to be here with."

Then he moved his fingers and bent his head, placing a kiss on the side of her mouth.

"You missed," she whispered as small breaths of anticipation escaped from her lips.

"I didn't miss Beth. When I kiss you next, it's going to be because you asked me to. I'm testing your management style."

With those words, he turned and left. She knew she had a silly grin on her face. She passed him in the field as she made it to her car. He nodded but said nothing else. As she drove to the hotel, all she could think about was Henry and his own management style.

Twelve

"I can't believe I'm here," Henry said to himself.

He walked down the hall of the courthouse where it opened out to a large room with five waiting chairs. The chairs were for the two office doors located in the room. Only one of them was occupied and Henry was here for that one. As he was approaching the door, it swung open.

"What do you want?"

"Jerry, I'm here to talk to you."

Jerry was dressed in his usual jeans and blue top. "You don't have an appointment. I don't know if I can see you."

Henry looked around the room. "There's no one here."

Jerry peeked around Henry and nodded. "You got the right of it, boy. Ain't no one in the room but it doesn't mean I don't have calls to take. Take a seat."

Henry nodded and then took a seat in the room. He tried to pick a chair that he thought would hold him. All of the wooden chairs looked old and as if they would break under the slightest pressure. He rested a knee on the chair closest to the door heard it start to give.

He immediately pulled his knee up. After that, he tested the other three until he found one that he thought would hold him.

"It's like playing goldilocks in the waiting room," he murmured to himself. About an hour later, the door flew open, and Jerry stepped into the waiting room. Henry stood up and smiled.

"I thought you'd be gone by now, boy."

"You said if I needed to talk, I could come by."

"I said that because my Geeta told me to. I never expected you to show up," Jerry complained.

"I didn't think I would be disturbing you."

"I have lots of work to do. When you get my age, sometimes getting out of bed and dressing yourself can be a feat. Besides, I'm too old to have to tell everyone what I do."

"I won't take too much of your time," Henry said.

"All of you say that, and it's never been true."

"Stay here and let me get my coat. If you are going to disturb me the least you can do is buy me a cup of coffee. I hear the coffee shop has cinnamon and spice."

Henry walked out with Jerry down the steps of the courthouse. When people said goodbye to Jerry, he grunted and gave him a look of pity and in some cases, relief.

"It seems like you have an odd relationship here at your work," Henry said, trying to start a conversation.

"Humph! There's nothing odd. I tell them the truth, and they need to decide if they want to hear it or not. But I always warn them not to ask me, though."

For Henry, it was a new experience to be walking down the streets of Sweet Blooms and not to have anyone talking about him. Just as Henry was about to try to talk to Jerry again, a young man approached. He stopped and hugged Jerry. It was the first time Henry had seen him show any outward affection toward anyone beside Geeta. It had been a while, but Henry was almost sure that the young man in front of him was Vihaan, Jerry's son.

Vihaan had thick hair and was dressed in a long green shirt and blue jeans. He had thick black hair that Henry thought must be a beast to keep in this weather and a ready smile that was so reminiscent of Geeta, it was easy to know who his mother was.

"Hello, you must be Henry," Vihaan said. He held out his hand to greet Henry. "I'm Vihaan, the son of this very chipper man. I'm sorry, I haven't had a chance to meet you. I heard that you are recently engaged. Congratulations"

Henry took Vihaan's hand and shook it. "As you said, I'm Henry Jenkins. I feel like we've heard about each other."

"I don't pay attention to gossip. I know that goes contrary to me saying I heard about your engagement, but I have a fiancée who would feel remiss if I didn't know the business of Sweet Blooms."

"No worries. I'm used to being in the spotlight, so I'm thrilled to be a side note."

"Is the old man keeping you on your toes?" Vihaan joked.

Henry grinned. "I'm not sure yet, he's a wily one."

"Don't worry, you're getting the public version of it all." Vihaan joked.

"The both of you are chattering like women. Vihaan, you go on to whatever you were doing."

Henry interrupted. "What I think he's trying to say

is that we are going to coffee, would you like to come?"

Vihaan looked at his dad, and then shook his head. "No, I won't interfere. I'm not a fan of cinnamon spice, right Dad?"

Jerry waved Vihaan off. "Go do something useful."

Henry noticed that Vihaan didn't even smart from Jerry's jab. Instead, he just bowed to Jerry and called over his shoulder. "I'll see you for dinner."

Finally, they walked into the coffee shop. When they arrived, the waitress seemed to know Jerry and took the order. Henry waited for Jerry to settle down. After the coffees arrived. Jerry was ready.

"What did you bother me for this time, we just spoke what seemed like a couple of days ago. Did you mess up in that time? That would be an impressive record if you did."

Henry looked at his coffee cup, unsure of where to start. This had seemed like a great idea when he was on the ranch but now.

"Boy, what rattled your cage so much you came looking for an old man like me?"

"Beth is an amazing woman."

"We covered that last time. Has she grown wings since the last time I saw her?"

"No."

"Well, then…"

Henry looked at Jerry and then blurted it out. "I don't think this is as fake as I thought it was."

"Ouch for you," Jerry said.

"I thought you would help me," Henry said.

Jerry looked up from his cup. "Help you with what Henry? Help you to realize that fake thing was the slowest thing you could have ever agreed to. Nope, couldn't do that. I have learned that youngun's don't listen. They have to burn their hands on the stoves themselves."

"I realized today that I need help talking to her."

"Does she speak English?"

"Yes, Jerry, she does."

"Are your words too simple, or does she use words you can't understand?"

Henry wanted to let his head fall to the table. "Let me be clear," Henry began.

"Yes, you should. I have to tell you if you talk to her this way, you really do need help talking."

"You've been with Geeta for more than ten years. You must know how to talk to women," Henry said.

Jerry looked up at him and then pushed the empty coffee cup away from him.

"If that's this is about, let me tell you how I talk to Geeta, and it may help you when you talk to Elizabeth. Every morning, I tell Geeta why I still love her and how I'll miss her through the day. At night when we go to sleep, I tell her how her love helped get me through the day.

"You see, it's not difficult. Just bare your soul to her, and all will be well."

"That's not really a plan, jerry," Henry said.

"It's the only plan you'll need if you're serious." With those words of wisdom, he got up, thanked Henry for the coffee and walked away.

Elizabeth closed the new crate in the barn. The miniature pincher was wrapped in a blue baby quilt. Dark eyes stared over the top of the quilt. This latest rescue had been brought in by her assistant, Calla. Calla was in her late sixties and was a retiree. She and Calla had met at an Adopt-a-Stray meeting, and they had become friends. She knew she would have to this Henry situation to her, but today was not the day.

Today when she got to her hotel room Calla was sitting in the lobby with a little bundle in her arms. She had brought the Min Pin out of the car and wanted to know if she should take him to the nearby shelter or if there was an open crate for her. The Min Pin was rescued from a puppy farm and was shivering and skittish. Elizabeth took one look at the dog and knew she would bring her to the barn. She didn't want the Min Pin to go to the shelter. Hearing all of those dogs, the Min Pin might think she was back at the farm. Elizabeth thought the Min Pin had gone through enough.

Elizabeth sent Calla to rest in the hotel, and she brought the Min Pin out to the barn to settle her in a quiet space.

"I see you've got a new resident," Henry said.

Elizabeth didn't acknowledge Henry right away. Instead, she made sure the Min Pin was settled, and she closed the door. She then stood up and faced Henry.

"This will be the first of many."

Henry stood against the door and gave her a slight nod of his head. *He must practice these poses*, she thought. It had to be practiced. When he leaned against the frame, it accentuated his chest and made the muscles on his arms bulge. Just when she thought she was going to do the right thing and stop ogling him, she lifted her gaze to his face *it just gets better* she thought. He had that five o' clock shadow that only nature could make. Well-defined cheekbones that led to a slightly crooked nose. Why hadn't she noticed that before? All of that wrapped up with a bow on it, because he had dark brown eyes that beckoned a woman to sink into his.

"It looked cute," he said as he pushed away from the doorway. "Will it be okay?"

"She's better now. A little shaken but in great shape considering what she's been through for the last four years."

"Was this the only rescue?"

Elizabeth shook her head. "No, she came from a puppy farm bust. She was so scared they didn't have the resources to take her in and watch her." Elizabeth stood up and brushed the dirt off of her hands. "The way information passes in this town, I'm surprised you couldn't tell me her story and my chief volunteer Calla's story too."

"Sorry, I don't know Calla, but if she stays here long enough, I'm sure I will."

"I'm sure you two will get along. She's pro animal rights, and when she meets you, she'll be thrilled with the way you care for your horses."

"I'm glad you think I'll pass muster."

Elizabeth smirked. "I'm sure you and Calla will be thick as thieves. In a lot of ways, Calla reminds me of Geeta. She has a way of making her own way in a place."

She didn't want to think about how she would have to explain to Calla what was really going on. She and Calla had been through so much applying for grants that it was only a matter of time before she explained how she managed this one.

"Come back to me," Henry said, reaching out to touch her on the shoulder. "Whatever you are thinking about, I can't keep up."

Elizabeth came out of her fog.

"Henry, what are you talking about?"

"What I'm saying is that whatever you were thinking about was really intense, and we have other things to work on. I don't like seeing your brow all scrunched up with worry. We can work on other things."

"We can?" Elizabeth said.

He walked up to her and placed two fingertips on her left shoulder and then traced her arm with his hand from her shoulder to her wrist.

"We've got to work on our engagement."

If Henry thought working on their engagement ruse was going to help the matter, he was going to be sadly mistaken. In fact, her having to think about the matter of them would make her life more stressful.

"What are we working on?"

Henry traced her arm back to her shoulder and then ran a light touch across her collarbone, up her neck and then to her chin.

"We're working on our engagement," he said in a low voice. "We need to get to know each other. We need to understand how we think. You know, to make sure this is authentic. We need to be a couple."

Elizabeth wasn't sure how this was going to work for Henry, but she could tell by the speeding up of her heart and the shortness of her breath that she was going to be more involved with Henry than she already was.

She tilted her head up to look into his eyes. It was a mistake. Instead of breaking the spell his voice had cast, she was falling deeper. In an attempt to break the spell, she tried to put some distance between them.

"What did you want to do, clean some crates together? You do know it's temporary, right?"

Henry smiled. "Me doing the crates or the engagement? I mean, I know I don't know a lot about dogs, but I didn't think I'd have to start with the crates."

She took a step back and shook her head, trying to clear the fog of him out of her mind so she could think again. "Stop playing, Henry."

His grinned got wider. "Elizabeth, I know you are amazing and fearless. We can do this."

She glared at him. "There shouldn't be so much to do. We smile when we are outside. We hold hands when we are walking down the street."

"That sounds like I'm one of the rescues. Certainly, engagement means more than that."

She was breathing through her nose and trying not to faint. How could words have such an effect on her? If his words put her off-kilter, what would spending more time with him do? What was she going to do?

"Did you want me to come by the hotel?"

"NO! I think meeting here is great. It's neutral ground, and we can work out neutral rules."

He nodded. "Yeah, what you said."

"I'll come over tomorrow, and we can discuss how we act in public." She was trying to think of how she could put it off longer, but this was all she could think of to delay.

"Did you name the latest rescue?" he asked.

Elizabeth shook her head. "Not yet."

"May I?"

Elizabeth was confused for a moment, and then it came together. "You want to name the Min Pin?"

She looked at him and smiled. Did men ask to name rescues? Her heart was filling up with the gushy, soft feeling that said Henry was the real thing. The sign that said he was a great catch. How many men would remember the rescue after she was out of sight?

"Okay, Henry, what do you want to name her?"

"That one's a no brainer. I want her to be called Wi-Fi."

Elizabeth looked at him with a curious expression. "Did you just say Wi-Fi?"

"Yes, I did."

"And the reason for this is?"

Henry walked up to Elizabeth, leaned in close as if he were going to kiss her, and then stopped right before touching her lips.

"Wi-Fi, because this is the day we started to talk to one another, and our engagement really began between us." He kissed her lightly on the lips and then walked away.

This could not be happening to her. What was it about that man? How did he do this to her? Elizabeth thought she was immune to all of the tricks and lures men put out, but Henry was a different beast on his own.

She needed to take today and figure out what she was going to do. She needed to calm down, and then it would all become clear. She walked over to the crates and check on all of the rescues until she was at Wi-Fi's crate.

She opened it up and scooped the dog into her arms. She saved senior dogs. She found places for them to go, and she never backed down or wondered if she could do it. She could handle Henry. The engagement was fake anyway. She'd never hook up with a man like Henry.

"You're on my side right, Wi-Fi. Guys are just trouble."

The Min Pin peeked above the blanket and then sank into the folds.

"Not a ringing endorsement, but I'll take it. Tonight we go home together, and tomorrow I'll deal with Mr. Henry."

Thirteen

Henry waited for Elizabeth in the barn. He'd covered the table with a cloth and had gone to Sweet Blooms Café for some breakfast muffins. He bought a carafe of coffee and had laid out the goodies under a net.

He knew it was time to do some serious wooing. The good news was Elizabeth wasn't totally immune to him. Well, he hoped that was the case. He could be patient to help her get past the trauma she had of being with a man who had lied to her. When he looked at Elizabeth, he saw hope for his tomorrow, and he was more than willing to wait on her.

He saw her coming towards the barn. She had a carrier in her hand as she approached. He wanted to go to her and take the carrier out of her hand, but he knew she'd probably fight him for it. He could tell the moment she spotted him. She stopped and gave him a once over that reminded him of a skittish mare he once had.

It still amazed him that this woman who wore sundresses and sandals could move him so. Her hair was back in a ponytail swishing with every step she took.

He didn't notice it until now, but she had no makeup on her face. One more way she told the world to accept her the way she was, or go away.

"Are you expecting guests?" she said as she put the carrier on the table.

"I'm hoping that an offering will make this process smoother," he said as he took off the net dome over the muffins.

A smile lifted her lips in a small grin. "Is this how you go about getting to know people, with subtle bribes?"

"This bribe wasn't subtle."

Elizabeth walked around to the other side of the table and looked at the unveiled treats. "I would love to indulge, but my conscious would haunt me. I don't think this getting to know each other thing is going to work."

"First, who says no to Sweet Blooms' muffins? Second, we're getting to know each other. We're not getting married."

He watched her look at the pastries and then at him. There was a grim set of determination in her eyes. Her body was stiff, and she looked as if she were bracing herself for something. He had expected some resistance, but he hadn't expected it to come this quickly or this strong.

"Listen, we're doing this for the grant. What does it matter what people think? Maybe we are giving this way too much attention, and that's why it's spiraling out of control. Getting to know me is a dead-end street. Why bother?"

"Why bother with getting to know you, and why does it matter what people think?"

She looked behind herself and then pulled a chair to the table. "I'm asking you it matters if we get to know each other? I don't think I can get to know a man right now, and I'm sorry to say, especially you."

"Ouch! Now we definitely need to eat some sugar."

Elizabeth rolled her eyes and then dropped her head into her hands. "I like you, Henry."

He looked over the muffins, trying to contain the internal fist pump that was going through his whole body. Then as soon as it came, a cold flow of reality washed over him. Maybe it was his past she didn't want to be associated with.

"Is it because I was married that I'm not the type of man you'd like to know?"

"No, it's not that. I think you are really brave to come back to the town where your ex is and try to make things right."

Then he stopped and looked at her before raising an eyebrow.

"Okay, so if it's not because of the divorce and you say you like me, what's the problem?"

She looked up from her hands and sighed. "You are the bad boy who left and then came back to redeem himself. You have all the makings of a hero Henry, even if you don't see it yet. You are a great example of what a man could do under the worst circumstances. We're in a town that dissects everything. I don't think my life can stand the scrutiny yours is under all the time."

He could feel the stress fading away from him as she spoke. "Do you think there is something in your past or something someone could bring up that I would judge you for?"

She stood up from the table and shook her head. "It's not worth going over history." She continued past him as if she were going to the crates. He stood up and stepped into her path.

"Beth," he whispered.

She wouldn't look at him. She wouldn't go around him. Finally, she lifted her head, and he saw the tremble of her lower lip and then anxiety that tore at his heart.

"Maybe," she whispered. "I think there was a time when money meant more than people, and I don't know if I can stand next to you or be put on display for a town to find that I was lacking. It's the lacking thing. I had to work a long time so I could see myself as whole and worthy. I can't take a town comparing me to their homegrown success case."

"I'm human, Beth. I've made mistakes too."

"I wanted to be with a man so much, and I wanted to be liked so much that I followed him even when I had second thoughts about what he was doing."

Henry caressed her cheek, enthralled by her scent and softness. "I'm not asking you to do something you don't agree with. I can't imagine you going along with just anything, either." He waited for her to argue. When she didn't, he dared to press on. "So what do you think? You think we can give it a try?"

She cocked her head to the side and then stepped away for a long moment. She gave him another look and then went to sit at the table. She looked back at Henry then.

"So you gonna make me eat all of these mini muffins by myself?" she asked.

Henry walked to the table and reached for a muffin.

"I'm going to do my share because I don't want to face the wrath of the Blooms. Those women can be brutal. I think you met one, Rose?"

She popped a muffin in her mouth. Henry went to pour them both coffees.

"You truly are a great asset to have around, if you come with muffins that is," she said as she grabbed another muffin and bit into it.

Henry had the coffee in his hand, and he was transfixed by her face. When she smiled, it lit up her face and gave her the glow of an angel. In those moments, when she smiled at him, he felt renewed and fresh. If she could smile at him after everything, then he could do anything. She didn't realize she had only to ask, and he'd find a way. He thought if he told her that now she'd run faster than his quickest thoroughbred.

Beth put all of herself into everything from the rescue to enjoying muffins. He could see her strength but wasn't deceived into thinking she wasn't soft.

He picked up a muffin and raised it as a toast. "To us getting to know one another," he said. He saw her hesitate for a moment, but she nodded and went along. "So, I was thinking we would start today?"

"Hold on, there. I can see your plan already. Giving me food and then throwing your ideas out there hoping I'll be to distracted by these delicious muffins."

"Is it working?"

"Almost, but my sense of survival is interfering with my food motivation."

"It's not going to be as invasive or bad as you might think. Let's start with what's important to us both and then we can go from there."

"Well, this is easy; the rescue is important to me. I'm

returning the favor of saving a life because Smiley saved me. If I had known that's all you wanted, I'd have said yes to getting to know you earlier."

Henry looked at her and smiled. "Beth."

She looked at him with an arched eyebrow. "You know the way you say Beth sounds like you are waiting for something else."

"You know that on top of us knowing things about each other, people will expect that we should be comfortable physically touching each other."

Elizabeth sat back. "Well, I think they should mind their business! What happens if you're not that kind of guy?"

Henry laughed. "What kind would that be?"

"You know, maybe you believe in waiting until we marry?"

"Beth, have you seen yourself in the mirror?"

Her hand went to her face. "Do I have muffin on my face?"

Henry stood up and went to Elizabeth. He held out his hand and stood up, so they were facing one another.

"Henry don't make a big production of it. If you see something on my face, just get to it."

"I asked about the mirror because no man who looks at you would ever think they could last without kissing you until we married. In fact, that would be a telltale sign that something was wrong.

"I'd like to kiss you, Beth. I'm asking to know if you're open to the idea."

"Of kissing? Now?"

"Yeah, that was the general thought. We'd kiss now and see how it goes."

"It's an in public kind of kiss, right?"

Henry saw her breath tick up, and her voice get lower. "I'm not sure what an in public kind of kiss is?"

"You know, the ones that are polite and not too involved."

"Ahh, those. We call those pecks."

"Pecks?"

"Yes, don't worry, we can start with pecks."

"Well, then go ahead."

She sounded like he was going to do punishment. He knew this was the first step to wooing Beth; it was just a little longer than maybe he thought. He leaned in and brushed his lips across hers. Apple, she'd eaten the apple muffin, and the taste of cinnamon and sugar was still on her lips.

He placed his hands on her hips and her breath hitched for a moment, then she relaxed. He pulled back and looked at her. Her eyes were closed, and her lips were waiting for him to take another taste. He leaned in again and lingered over her lips until he felt her hands reach up and rest on his shoulders. It took all of his self-control not to pull her closer and deepen the kiss, but he remembered this was about the long game and winning Beth, not the temporary one of enjoying the moment.

When he lifted his head this time, her eyes were wide open, and a smile was on her lips. He was about to lean in again when a person yelled out Henry's name.

"Who is that, and do you have to go?" Beth asked.

Henry didn't release her. "It's Joe, the mailman. His hearing is going so he yells out and usually if I'm close I'll go to him. Today I think I'm going to have to pass on talking to the mailman. My hands are full."

He saw the blush spread across her face as she turned away and looked at his arms about her.

"I think that was a bit more than a peck."

"It's a sign, Beth."

She looked at him with a narrowed gaze. "It's a sign of what?'

He grinned. "It's a sign that I'm going to need to work on our communication. I mean, if we can't even agree on what's a peck and what isn't, how is our marriage going to go?"

She gave him a smile and turned to the table. "Let's eat. We can both agree on that. The rest we'll work on."

Fourteen

The devil was in the details. Henry looked at the documents in front of him and then pushed them around his desk some more. No matter what he did, his eyes kept falling to the document that would break Beth.

He was in a small shed that had been temporarily converted into an office. It had two rooms. The largest room was his office, and the smaller room outside was the coffee room and waiting room. After looking at the document all afternoon, he needed a break.

As he got to his door, the door to the shed opened, and in came his friend Jason Conners. Jason was Henry's friend, lawyer, and contact to the business world if need be. He practiced law, but was truly an artist who did freelance paintings and sculptures on the side. Jason told him it was to keep his sanity while he toiled in law.

Henry had seen Jason's work and had told him to go full-time, but Jason always brushed him off. When Henry had told Jason he was coming back to Sweet Blooms, Jason had praised him and told him he was doing the right thing.

"Are you still glad that you came out to Sweet Blooms?" Henry asked as he saw his friend walk over to the coffee pot.

"It's given me time to work on some pieces that I wanted to," Jason said.

"Then why the dragging feet?"

"It's given me time because there is nothing to do in this town. You can't get mad at them for gossiping, I think that's the only event that is still open after nine."

Henry grinned. "You wanted to concentrate."

"I could concentrate in solitary confinement as well, but you don't see me signing up for that, do you?"

"You could have told me that you would only do teleconferences."

Jason ran his hand through his blonde, spiked hair.

"I could have, but you so rarely ask me for anything that I had to show up."

"Could it be that you're saying I'm not a consistent pain to you?"

Jason smirked at him. "Not at all. You are still the most troublesome client I have, but in this, you wouldn't have been outside of your right to request that I show up."

Jason was an inch shorter than Henry, and he had signature blue eyes. He was dressed like every day was a surfing day, and Henry didn't know if Jason owned any shirts that could cover all of the tattoos he had on his body. What amazed Henry was Jason was as skilled a lawyer as he was a sculptor. Jason had saved him legally on more than one occasion.

Henry went to the coffee pot just in time for Jason to pour a cup. "I read the papers you left for me."

"What do you want to do with it?"

Henry smiled. "I was hoping to get your input." The ramifications of the papers weren't lost on him; he just wasn't sure the best way to go.

"What's the problem? Do you know what you want as a goal?" Jason asked.

Henry nodded.

"Well, then half of the problem is solved. I told you I was suspicious about the grant thing from the beginning. Elizabeth Butler signed this grant under the false premise that you and her own the land jointly."

"The grant doesn't say that," Henry interjected.

"It's true. The grant is very vague. If she had read the sub subsections, she would have found that whoever's name is on the deed is who owns the land and who owns the sanctuary. When she puts those animals on your land, you will essentially own everything and would be able to tell her to go away. It seems like that would be the best option, yes?"

"Jason, things have gotten complicated. First, I don't want a sanctuary, so I have no intention of taking her pride and joy from her. In fact, if all goes well, I'm hoping she'll wind up with my name as well."

"Wow, that was quick!" Jason said. "I mean, that's one way to help her. I never knew you were so giving."

"Don't be a smart aleck."

"Me? I don't know Henry, maybe I need to leave right away. I mean, you've been back a couple of months, and now you're telling me the woman who approached you for a nonprofit deal, which she probably had to say she owns part of, if not all of your land, is who you want to marry. You know this is what happens when everything closes at nine in a town."

"Beth is different. When you meet her, you'll understand," Henry said.

"So, the smitten always says. Listen, I have some rules in my life. I don't do drugs. I don't do married women, and I don't do marriage. It's a fifty-fifty hit or miss with those. They either kill you or change you for the rest of your life."

"I'll be here when your day comes."

"You'll be waiting a long time, my friend," Jason said with a smile. "Okay, so now that you've determined that you've found 'The One' what else is bothering you."

"There is a mention of Lance Classon," Henry said.

Jason nodded. "Yeah, that one was a little odd. It seems as though on the original paperwork files that Mr. Classon had listed the address of the sanctuary on some property upstate that belonged to him. The grant money will go to the landowner. I'm not sure when your gal decided to change the address, but she didn't tell Mr. Classon. There's someone name Mr. Zecky who had to inform Mr. Classon he wouldn't be getting the funding. Mr. Zecky's notes are very detailed."

"Jay, what's your thought on it?"

"My thought is Mr. Classon was about to take the money and run. The property he listed has been in foreclosure for some time. If any money had been sent I doubt he would have used it to pay back the amount owed, there's too big a difference."

"I've met Mr. Classon," Henry admitted. "He didn't strike me as the kind of guy who would be open and helpful to the cause. The real question is how much to tell Beth?"

Henry sipped his coffee and tried to look at the issue with some objectivity. He was just getting close to Beth.

She had so much distrust, and looking at this situation, he could see that it was justified. He didn't want to lose the ground he had gained with her by bringing this all up.

Jason sighed. "And this is one of the main reasons I won't be falling in love. Your ability to think is seriously impaired. Listen, if you are going to be with her anyway, you can just wait until you're married and give it to her as a gift then."

"What if she finds out before?"

Jason laughed. "I'm your friend and your lawyer. Your lawyer is advising you not to say a thing. What happens if she turns out to be a gold-digger? I mean, she already started on the wrong foot with this grant. So giving it to her when you are ready to marry her is a safe bet that I can endorse. However, as your friend, let me tell you, secrets always come out. Tell her.

"Okay, that's enough for me. All this talking about relationships and honesty is making me nervous. I just wanted to make sure you didn't have any questions. Now, I'm going to find some waves to relax."

Jason left out of the shed. Henry thought about earlier today in the barn and how hesitant Beth had been. He made a decision he'd tell her. He just needed to find the right time.

Lance Classon looked at the steps to the courthouse and snickered to himself. "Country folk." He couldn't imagine what made Elizabeth come to this town. He looked at his Armani suit and knew he looked good. *Appearances have to be kept,* he thought. Although looking at this town, maybe it wasn't as important as he thought.

He needed to see Clarissa Hastings-Parcel. Save for the Cades, it seemed as though she would be the only one to understand what was important, money. He was pleasantly surprised when he made it to her office, and the little number who was sitting outside of the office wasn't too hard on the eyes. He didn't give her more than a customary smile when she opened the door and let him into Clarissa's office.

The office was country chic, maybe. The furniture had throws on it that seemed handmade. The carpet was surprisingly Persian. The walls were decorated with expensive frames but had different photos in them. Some of the photos were amateur shots of people laughing, and the others appeared to be works of art he'd expect in a museum. In the room was a couch with a coffee table in front of it, and to his left her desk, which dominated the room with its rich oaks and detailed engravings.

"Hello Mr. Classon, please come in and take a seat. I'm interested in why you came to see me."

Clarissa was just as beautiful as the pictures made her out to be. Lance had been around women enough to know which ones needed their makeup and which one's make-up was just an afterthought. Clarissa didn't need her makeup at all. Her blonde hair was pulled up in a bun that gave full view of her almond-shaped eyes and full lips. This was a woman any man would be happy to have on his arm. He could see from the Versace dress she wore he had been right in coming to see her.

"I'm in town, and it would be a shame to not see the famous wife of Bain Parcel. I can tell you your beauty wasn't exaggerated."

Clarissa sat back in her high-back chair and

laughed. It was a full laugh that Lance thought was inappropriate for a woman.

"Be careful, Mr. Classon, your armor is cracking," she purred.

Lance tried to keep his lips straight, but he could tell he had made a mistake when Clarissa looked at him with a raised eyebrow and then tapped the side of her mouth.

"Mr. Classon, it's that little twitch that's giving you away. I don't have all day, and this isn't a social call, so why don't you tell me what you want and I'll tell you if you can have it."

"There is an Elizabeth Butler in town."

"Yes, I know her. I also know that you two were once involved but are no longer."

"Elizabeth has always been mercenary. She asked me to help her set up her sanctuary. I gave her money and put my own land in foreclosure, believing she was going to set up the sanctuary on my land."

"Have you spoken to her since you've been here?"

"Yes, yes. I couldn't come right away, but as soon as work permitted, I came. It may not seem like it, but I didn't want another person to be duped into putting out money and setting up things only to have her bail on them too."

"You're here for someone else's sake, Mr. Classon? I might have a bit of trouble buying that one."

Lance was confused. "Mrs. Parcel, what have I done to make you distrust me?"

Clarissa leaned forward and looked him in the eye. "I think Lance, you don't mind if I call you Lance, do you?"

He nodded.

"I think it was the way you came into my office and assigned a dollar value to everything you saw. It was the way you looked around my office but took a double-take of the Persian Rug on the floor. It was a gift from my husband, by the way, he knows I like to walk barefoot in my office. It's always the little things that give people away."

Lance sat back and re-evaluated the situation. "You've been upfront with me so let me return the favor, Clarissa is it?"

"It is, and you may not address me by it. Mrs. Parcel will do."

"I came here because I wanted to know if she was going to hang me to dry with the bills. I had hoped to find someone who would understand and, if possible, to stop her from scamming someone else. If you look at the paperwork, you'll see how we originally set it up. You're right; I didn't follow for someone else's good. I came to see if she would do the right thing and honor her agreement with me."

He watched Clarissa sit back in her chair. She was smart and beautiful. It was a shame she was married to Bain.

"I'll look over the record, and I'll get back to you, Mr. Classon."

She didn't say anything else, and Lance felt as though he was being dismissed. Instead of lashing out and telling her how she was wasting her life in this little town, he stood up and bowed.

"Thank you for your time. I'll be waiting to hear from you."

Fifteen

"We're going to play a game," Henry said, as the both of them sat down on the blanket he had laid out by the pond.

Elizabeth took a seat and looked at him with a grin. "So, do you bring all of your women out here to the pond?"

"Beth, you are like no other woman I've met. I won't tell you, you are the only one I've ever brought here, but the last one I brought here was when I was sixteen, and Mable Lee was an older woman of eighteen years."

Elizabeth turned to him and burst out laughing. "Now how can I compare to that?" she said.

Henry had left a message with her on the phone, asking if she would stay a little longer so they could begin getting to know one another. She was exhilarated and nervous at the same time. The memory of this morning was still on her lips.

When she had read his text this afternoon, it had done nothing to remove the memory. Elizabeth was already questioning her sanity in trusting a man so soon. Just because he made her laugh and made her feel like a woman again didn't mean she should throw caution to the wind. In fact, if she said it long enough, she'd start to believe it.

Now that the moment was here and she was sitting in front of Henry, she couldn't really recall why she was so nervous in the first place. This was Henry. What she saw was what she got, and she could trust him.

While she sat, he unpacked some containers of food and a small wicker basket with a top on it. She couldn't remember the last time a man had gone out of his way to share a special place with her. When he had mentioned that she wasn't the first one he'd brought, she wanted to jump up and go home. Then he defused the whole situation by telling her about Mable Lee and then she realized how silly she was being. She was looking for a reason to run. She wouldn't let fear ruin her chance at finding happiness. She decided then that Henry was worth trusting.

He pulled out multicolored plastic glasses that looked as if they had been purchased at the dollar store. Then he pulled out a carafe from the basket and poured them both a drink. It smelled sweet. She could see it was a light pink and had bubbles in it. When she took a sip, it tickled her nose, and she looked up at him.

"Is this a Shirley temple?"

He smiled at her. "I pulled out all the stops for you. This fine glassware and a nice girly drink."

"A girly drink?"

"You know it's kind of wine-like and classy, but something I can't drink outside of this pond area."

She tried to hold back her grin, but she could feel it spread across her face. "No Shirley temples in public then. It will be our little secret."

Henry smiled. "See, we're already sharing secrets about one another."

"So this is your idea of romantic?"

"Ouch! For a woman who wasn't sure she wanted to get to know me too, I'm missing the mark."

Elizabeth stared at him and found herself relaxing into his voice. When he spoke, it was animated and sure. He made her feel cared for and special by asking her what she wanted to eat, removing her garbage when she was done, and refilling her glass when it was empty.

"So how long before you tell me what's in that wicker basket?"

Henry pointed at the basket. "Oh, this thing here? I didn't even think you noticed it."

She looked at him and smirked. She was leaning on her side when he brought the wicker basket to the middle.

"I noticed. What's in it?"

"This is the beginning of our getting to know each other."

She sat up and looked at him sideways. "Come again?"

He opened the basket, and inside were slips of paper. "It's a game. We'll ask three questions each. If you think the other person has answered truthfully, then the next person goes. If you think they didn't, say Challenge, and if they're right, the person can claim a forfeit."

"This sounds like truth or dare, and I've never liked that game," she said.

"It sounds like you're finding new ways to back out of getting to know me."

Elizabeth was sitting up now, and her hands were in her lap. "Only three questions, right?" she said skeptically.

"On my word, three questions."

"Fine, let's do it. Who goes first?" she asked.

"Ladies, of course."

She reached in and picked out a question. "Name a moment you were proud of?"

Henry looked at her and then sat up straighter. "One of the proudest moments in my life was when they told me that Nathan had been born healthy. Hannah had been sick through the pregnancy. Money had been scarce. My father had left my mom for weeks on end when she was sick. He used to practically run away from her when she was sick. I know now he was afraid and felt helpless, but I was so proud that I hadn't done what my dad had done. I hadn't left her when she was sick."

Elizabeth stared at Henry and wondered again about the depths of this man. He caught her gaze. "Your turn, what was one of the proudest moments in your life?"

She cleared her throat and then looked up at the sky before smiling. "The day I received my first check. I must have been sixteen on a part-time job. I was working as a cashier, and I was horrible at it," Elizabeth smiled as she remembered. "The first week I received my check, I didn't even cash it right away. I made a photocopy of it and carried it around in my pocket, even after I cashed it."

"So, making your own money is important?" Henry asked.

"It's not the money. It's the idea of having something that no one can take away from you."

Henry's smile faltered for a moment, and then he

reached into the basket. "Name a person you admire, and why?"

Elizabeth waited. "I can't wait to hear this one."

Henry grinned. "The person I admire the most is Jerry. You met him he was on the—"

"He was on the council. Yes, I remember him. He was outspoken and direct," she said.

Henry nodded. "That would be Jerry all of the time. When I was growing up, he was always around. He gave me advice. It was never anything I wanted to hear. I would always say 'I'm not going back to that old man,' but when I needed an honest answer, he gave it. The other thing about Jerry is he has the life I've always wanted."

"Really?"

"Jerry is married to Geeta. They have both endured a lot, and it's made them stronger. They still love each other, and they are still best friends. I don't think it gets any better."

After a moment of silence, Henry spoke. "Your turn. The person you most admire."

Elizabeth sniffed and thought back. "The woman I most admire is a person who goes by the name of mother. I met her in a shelter. I had just lost everything, and I found myself alone and in a shelter. In the beginning, I thought she was crazy, but as time went on, she took me under her wing and helped me to make it until Smiley came along and gave me purpose.

She was living on the street because she was healing herself. It wasn't the way her family wanted it to be, but it was working for her, and she was happy with it. I learned a lot from her in a short amount of time."

Elizabeth sniffed and shook her head.

"Sorry, I'm putting a damper on the mood."

"No, Beth, this is the point. It's never a downer learning about you."

She looked in the basket and pulled out the last one. "What was your most memorable kiss?"

She looked at him and shook her head. "Really?"

"Hey, I think I did really good with my questions. Don't beat me for being me."

"Fine, my most memorable kiss was at my sixth-grade graduation. In the town I was in, it was a big deal to go from the elementary school to the middle school. They had a mini graduation, and we all got dressed up for it.

"Anyway, we couldn't have dates, but I met Michael Polesty, and we went into the stairway, and he said to me. 'Elizabeth we're going to middle school, and I think I want you to be my girlfriend.'"

Henry laughed. "He told you?"

"Oh yes, Michael was very confident for all of his eleven years. Anyway he reached out to me with puckered lips. I saw his lips, and they just looked gross. I tried to call his name, but he didn't listen. Instead, he leaned forward. I leaned back, and then we both toppled down three steps."

"What happened then?"

"The teacher came in and told Michael this was the third girl he had been caught with and that he would be getting a letter to his parents. The teacher also told me that I'd be lucky not to get pregnant. So when I went into the party, I worried the whole party if I was pregnant."

"Really?"

"Yes, Michael had fallen on top of me, and I was all-knowing then."

"Then?"

"Okay, Mr. Know-It-All, your go."

"This shouldn't come to you as a surprise."

"Yes?"

"Challenge."

He leaned over the basket and kissed her. They weren't touching, and she could pull back at any moment. The distance gave her the freedom to enjoy the moment. The feelings rushed through her and then swirled around her, cocooning her in a warmth that made her lean into him.

The kiss wasn't demanding. He enticed her with easy movements and made subtle promises with this kiss if she wanted to stay. As she angled herself to get closer, she felt the brush of his hand against her neck. The warmth that had surrounded her before centered low in her stomach and began to stoke as if it were a furnace being fed.

Just when she was ready to reach out and pull him closer, she felt a cool breeze against her lips. Where his hand had been, the warmth was fading. Henry had pulled back and was sitting on his haunches, looking at her. His breathing was a little rapid, and she thought he would lean in again, but then he began to pack.

He looked at her and gave her a tremulous smile. "It's time I took you home, Beth."

She was confused. "I don't—"

"It was a challenge and a game. What happens between us will be because of vows, commitment, and love if we're lucky. I want to do the right thing, so I need to step back and cool down."

She nodded. "I can get myself back to the hotel."

Henry was about to protest. "I'm fine. I need time to think about this, as well."

Henry nodded. "Thank you, Beth."

"For?"

"For giving me the most memorable kiss of my life."

She smiled at him and began the walk to her car. The only thing that kept ringing in her head was, *Oh my goodness, I think I've fallen for Henry Jenkins.*

Sixteen

"You have once again attracted a great group of trainees," Calla said. She looked at Elizabeth and smiled. "I noticed the classes started out with a large number of single women and then thinned noticeably."

Calla was there because it was time to make some decisions about Sweet Inspirations and she had been ribbing Elizabeth on this all week. Clarissa came to make sure they stayed within code, and then Calla would go over staffing.

"Listen," Elizabeth said, "it's not about the age or the marital status. I want to make sure my dogs are getting the best care by the most qualified people. The dogs have to be the priority."

"I think she just ran around the block to say yes she has removed the women who applied so they could try to steal away Henry," Clarissa said with a grin.

"It's not about me; it's always about the dogs," she replied.

Calla reached out. "No one is saying you don't do the right thing. I know I rag on you a lot, but you're doing the right thing. I was a little skeptical when the teens applied, but it turns out they were pretty good."

Calla's home goods were on their way. She still hadn't found a place to live, but it didn't seem to bother her. She was a lot like Elizabeth. It was about the dogs first.

So here they were meeting in the lobby of the hotel Elizabeth was staying in. Elizabeth was more of a silent observer. This was a duty she would back out of, and Calla and Clarissa would have to handle between themselves. The process would begin after a candidate applied. Then they'd go through the training with her. If they pass, they do an interview with Calla, and then Calla and city council members go over the candidates. It allowed Calla to find out if any of the candidates had DUI's, or if they may need some additional help to work at the ranch.

After all of the volunteers were discussed, Clarissa said she had an additional item to bring up.

"I know this is going to seem odd to both of you, but Sweet Blooms is a small town, and most of us know one another. As a result, we watch out for each other. I want to talk about Henry," Clarissa said.

"Well, thank goodness, because I want Elizabeth to talk about Henry as well," Calla said.

Elizabeth looked at both women and knew she was going to have to say something.

"He's been very open about the use of space. He's assisted whenever I've asked him. When the volunteers are distracted, he doesn't encourage their behavior, and he's generally good to have around in case I have any questions."

"Well, if we're talking about the dry, business stuff, he was good with me, too, when I did my interview. He appeared to be responsible."

Clarissa tapped her nails on the armrest. "If I wanted to know the weather or his job qualifications, I could have pulled that. I want to know if you and Henry are in some type of a relationship," Clarissa said.

Elizabeth knew neither one of them would be deterred. "The terms of the land say we need one owner and not two. For a certain amount of time, we will be engaged to make sure we fulfilled the letter of the grant."

"You know we can find another grant? We don't need to take this one," Calla said. At that moment, Elizabeth loved Calla even more.

Elizabeth reached out and touched her hand. "Thanks, but I think this will work," Elizabeth said and then turned to Clarissa, who was watching her intently.

"Well, I'll say this does put a wrinkle in an item or two. Tell me, Elizabeth, are you aware that a Lance Classon is in town as well?"

Elizabeth nodded. "He's here, but he'll go as soon as he realizes there's no money to be made." Even though everyone nodded, Elizabeth could feel her temper rising. She was always explaining as if she needed supervision all the time. She knew Clarissa and Calla were trying to help her, but it chaffed for her to think they thought they had to have this conversation with her.

"Well, we've got the surface things together. Are you aware of what the town will say about Henry?" Clarissa asked.

"I'm not really sure why they need to say anything," Elizabeth fired back.

Clarissa smiled. "You asking that question just means you've never lived in a small town. I get it can be confining, but at the end of the day, we look out for each other."

Calla leaned over and placed her hand on Clarissa's arm.

"Did you see that immediate defense she sprang too?" Calla said to Clarissa.

"I'm glad I caught it." Clarissa responded. "It means she's already falling for Henry."

Elizabeth stared at both of the women in the conversation. She couldn't believe they were talking about her and Henry as if this was going to be a town decision and not a decision between Henry and her.

Clarissa stood up. "Well, it's been a great meet and greet. I have what I came for."

"And what was that, Clarissa?" Elizabeth asked.

"I came to make sure the town people were being treated fairly. Henry is the classic prodigal son, but he's Sweet Blooms' prodigal son. Now I have business. Elizabeth, care for Henry."

"It's only temporary," grumbled Elizabeth.

Clarissa laughed as she stood to leave.

"Keep saying that to yourself, Elizabeth. Maybe if she say it enough Calla, she'll start to believe it."

Lance saw Elizabeth in the lobby and waited until her friends left. He knew she probably wouldn't meet with him unless he caught up to her. Trying to meet her at the ranch was a no go if Henry was there.

Henry. As if he were a better option than Lance?

Lance wanted to make sure he didn't make the same mistakes he had made with Clarissa. He didn't know what had gone wrong. Elizabeth always used to take his advice and do what he said. Now, he needed her to obey just once more.

After all of the women had left, he gave it another two minutes, and then he went to approach her.

"Finally, a chance to talk to you," he said as he sat down in the still warm chairs of the women she had been meeting with.

"Lance, what do you want?" she said, resigned.

"No pleasantries Elizabeth? Even after what we meant to each other?"

Elizabeth put her arms over her chest and gave Lance a level stare.

"No, there are no pleasantries to exchange or give because we didn't end on good terms."

He had planned so much for them. Elizabeth always had those innocent features. There were new scams where he could use an innocent face, and Elizabeth fit the bill.

"Let's move beyond that Elizabeth, and work on today."

He saw her jaw lock and twitch, and then she pulled herself together. "Fine, Lance, what is it that you want?"

"I just want to talk. I thought this grant thing was already good to go on the first property Mr. Zechy showed you?"

He saw her look at him, but it didn't matter now. He had to get some money to get that program back to his property.

"We were going to go there, but my helper Calla didn't think the change in weather in New York would be good for the dogs. She reached out, and the nearby rescue was going to ask for funding. When the idea was presented to the council, they approved the setup of our nonprofit, and they granted some additional funding to the rescue. It was a win-win."

Lance nodded his head and took mental notes. He didn't actually think of the simple creatures. At the end of the day, they were just dogs.

"Well, I can see that you made a sound financial decision."

"Thank you. I don't need your approval on my transactions, but it's nice to hear something positive from you."

He looked around and then decided he had to let her know now. "Well, that's not completely true."

"What's not exactly true? What are you talking about, Lance?"

Lance watched Elizabeth, and some of his confidence started to come back. She was unsure of the statement she made, so she tightened up in the chair. Her body was stiff, and as long as it made sense, he could guide her to doing just about anything.

"What I'm saying is that I found you the land, but you decided not to take it after it had been taken off the selling block."

"Well—I,"

"Come, come, Elizabeth. We both know that I did some work. It's true you didn't use it, but I still put time and effort into it. I think I'm due to be reimbursed for my time."

"Time and effort? You want me to pay you for time and effort?"

"Elizabeth, I'm not asking for a ten percent deposit for the land which, had you dealt with anyone else, you would have had to give them in a deposit. If you had decided on another property, they still would have kept the deposit."

Lance saw Elizabeth hesitate and knew it was time to go in for the kill.

"If you don't want to give me my share, I can always ask Henry. That's his name, right, Henry?"

He saw her thinking at the table, and he gave her the extra time to work things out. "How much money are you talking about?"

"Well, the tract of land was worth $150,000. So I'd want ten percent of that and another ten percent for my time."

Elizabeth stood up. The sudden gesture took Lance by surprise.

"I'll see what I can do. I'm not promising anything," she said.

Lance nodded and remained calm on the outside, but inside he was jumping like a flea.

"I'm not asking for extra here, Elizabeth. I just want my fair share is all I'm asking for."

She gave him one more nod. "Listen to me, Lance. I can't guarantee a thing. I'm just saying I'll try."

He nodded and watched as Elizabeth walked away. He was already thinking of the next reason he could come up with to convince Elizabeth to give him more money.

Seventeen

"I don't know what I ever saw in him," Elizabeth grumbled before taking another slice of pizza. "He seems to always have that smug look on his face like he knows something that I don't. It drives me crazy."

Henry sat across from her on the blanket. They had fallen into the habit of coming to the pond to talk. Now it was their place, and every time they came, she was more and more relaxed.

"Well, I don't know what you saw in him either. I mean, he's not me," he said.

She stopped with the slice midway to her mouth and smiled at him before taking a bite. She took a couple of chews and then wiped her mouth with a napkin.

"Can you believe the gall he has? If I had been thinking straight instead of doubting myself, I would have told him to take a leap."

"Well, then I guess we should be really happy that you were a little slow yesterday."

Elizabeth stopped and looked at Henry. "You know you are being really sweet, letting me vent about Lance."

"My sweetness has an ulterior motive."

"And that is."

"I want to make sure you know that you can vent to me about anything. Including that dastardly devil Lance," he said as he twirled an imaginary mustache and spoke in a very bad German accent.

"Why didn't I challenge him? I knew what he said was fishy at best. I also know that Lance loves money and will say or do anything to get it, but when he was talking, for a moment, I was unsure."

Henry picked up a slice. "Stop beating yourself up. You have to remember that there was a time when you would do anything for him. You had feelings for this person. It's hard to let those feelings go. It's hard to admit that you were wrong."

"You seem like you have a good insight into the things other people think. You don't think I was mean because I didn't tell him no right away?"

Henry finished his pizza and took a little longer on the last chew. As he did, he wrapped his arms around his stomach and rocked back and forth. Exaggerating how tasty the pizza was by slowly rubbing his stomach.

"Really, Henry? It wasn't that good."

Then he stopped and smiled at her. "Got you to think about something else."

She smiled. "Yes, you did, but now I'm thinking about it again, so answer the question."

"The short answer is you are a very kind person to even be worried about him. He's a big boy, and if he plays in business, then he knows things don't always work out." He looked at her as she seemed to roll it over in her mind.

"So let's talk about your day yesterday. Anything new and exciting happen?"

Henry thought this would be the time to tell her. Then he looked at her smiling face and how she was just talking about how Lance wanted something from her, and he couldn't bring himself to do it. He'd have to go back to Jason and get him to move on getting the paperwork done for her.

"I met with my lawyer yesterday, and we went over some decisions I have to make now that I'm staying here. He basically reviews all of my dealings and then meets with me to make sure that I understand what's going on."

"Was it okay?"

Henry hesitated, and for a moment, he thought this might be a good time. Then when he opened his mouth, something different came out.

"Jason brought an issue to my attention, and I was a little conflicted about it. My instincts said one thing, but I think I was afraid to do that, so I chose option B."

She looked at him for a moment. "I would have never thought you were the type of person who would ever doubt what you were doing."

"It happens, Atlas, I can not be amazing at all things," he said in a French accent.

"Well, next week I'll be putting you to the test. The builders will be coming out to start the crate house, and a landscaper will come out to make dog trails."

Henry looked at the way her eyes lit up, and she was so enthusiastic as she explained the layout of the ranch and how it would all work together. By the time she was done, he was caught up in the excitement as well.

"I can see you've put a lot of thought into this and what the dogs will need," he said.

"You know senior dogs are so often overlooked. As if

their best days are behind them. When Smiley found me, I felt the same way. I thought I'd never be able to hold my head up again. I thought the end was just lurking around the corner. I want to be able to give back what Smiley gave to me."

He looked into her eyes, which were blinking to hold back unshed tears.

"I want you to know how much I admire you. You saw something that everyone else overlooked, and you decided to do something about it. It makes me glad I'm engaged to you. Maybe some of those good habits will rub off."

"Rub off?" she asked, with a laugh.

Then he reached across and touched her cheek with the back of his hand. She leaned towards his caress and then held his hand to her cheek.

"So we haven't done a getting to know you exercise today," Henry said.

She pulled back and sat on her butt. "Really? We have to do that?"

"Wow, we're not even married, and you're already tired of me? This doesn't bode well for us," he said.

"Okay, okay, what do you want to know now? What my favorite food is? Or what is my oldest secret?"

He looked at her and shook his head. "Beth, describe me."

He saw her blink and then go blank. "What?"

"You heard me, describe me," he said with a laugh.

"Well, well, you look like…you look like you, Henry. This is silly. Okay, you go first so I can see."

"I think that's dodging," he said.

"It's not dodging. You're just upset you didn't think of it first."

Henry laughed. "I did, which is why I asked you to go first." When he saw she was about to respond, he held up his hands. "I will go first. Just don't hurt me."

"Okay silly, go ahead."

He lay back on the blanket and looked up at the trees.

"You're not going to look at me?"

"Beth, I don't need to. This is how I see you. You are just the right height to look me in the eye. It's true you'd have to go up on those tropical colored toes of yours, but you could do it. You're leggy too. I can tell when you wear those sundresses. Every time you take a step, I can see the outline of your calves. Your calves are shapely and firm. It reminds me that besides being beautiful, you are strong and athletic.

"Your waist is small. I know that because I've seen you tote those senior dogs on your hips, and they fit on your hip as if you made a carved out place for them. Your hands are manicured and soft. I know you keep your nails short so you don't hurt the dogs. You're like that, giving to everything and everyone around you. I can see that kindness in your eyes and on your face.

"Your face I could look at all day long. Every emotion and thought you have runs across your face. When you're happy, you smile wide enough to show that one dimple on your cheek. When you're angry, your lips are clamped tight, and your cheeks kinda sink in. When you're sad, you fill your cheeks with air, and your eyes are downcast. Yes, Beth, I know what you look like."

Henry opened his eyes and looked over at Beth. She was sitting with a look of wonder on her face.

"That's what you see?"

"That and more."

She began to lean towards him when her cell phone rang.

"You could ignore it," Henry said.

Then the ringtone began, and the song Stand By me began to play. She turned and reached for her phone. "I've got to answer it. It's Calla."

Henry looked at her as concern and fear ran across her face. When she was done, she closed the phone and stood up.

"I've got to go. Calla says she has Smiley, and he's not feeling well."

"You want me to come?"

"No, he's old, so it's probably a false alarm. I'll let you know, and Henry?"

"Yes?"

"I just wanted you to know. I've never felt so beautiful as I did when you described me. Thank you."

Eighteen

Elizabeth walked into the lobby of the hotel and saw Henry sitting in a large chair, tapping his feet. He had a box labeled Sweet Blooms. He had the best timing. She walked up to him and gave him a tremulous smile. He had told her yesterday that he could see all of her emotions on her face. She wondered if that was true and what he would see today.

"Morning, slash afternoon," he said. "I wanted to talk to you, and I thought I'd bring a peace offering to make up for the rudeness of just showing up."

"You don't need a peace offering but I appreciate it none-the-less," she said. She thought he would give her the box, instead, he bent down and gave her a kiss. It wasn't a deep kiss but it was unexpected. She was happy that she hadn't pulled away or jumped.

Then she reached for the box.

"Kisses are nice, but sweets are sweets." She sat down and took her first bite. Elizabeth felt that something was off, but she couldn't pinpoint what.

"How's Smiley?" he asked. She had just come from the vet, and the news was still fresh in her mind.

"Yesterday, Smiley wasn't eating. Smiley loves to eat.

Calla took him to the doctor, and they found a lump pushing on his stomach. They don't know what it is, but they have to remove it. He's going to go into surgery today. When they go in, they'll take a biopsy and find out if the lump is cancerous or not."

"I'm sorry, I didn't know and when I saw you—"

"I already cried all last night with Calla. I lay with Smiley in the kennel as well. When I woke up this morning I was determined to have only positive thoughts. I can't even begin to imagine what life would be like without Smiley. I know that may not make me very mature, but it's the best I can do right now."

Henry opened his arms, and she went into them. She was glad that she could hide her face in his shoulder. She was scared the tears would come, and if they did she wouldn't be able to stop them. Elizabeth's plans when these things happened were to always focus on someone else.

When she first came into the lobby she could see something had been bothering Henry but she couldn't figure out what. Now it was moot. She was in his arms and after the long night she just wanted to relax in his arms. When his hands started to move up and down her back she settled even more into his arms.

There was something about Henry that disarmed her, pulled her in and gave her the feeling of being safe and cherished.

"I'm here for you if you need me Beth," he said. "I'm sure Smiley will be fine but no matter what happens, I'll be here for you."

"Thank you. Calla offered to do my meetings for the day but I needed to move around. If I had stayed with Smiley at the vet I think I would have been done before he came out of surgery."

He pulled back and tucked a strand of hair behind her ear.

"Hey, all of the dogs are fighters, from Smiley to Wi-Fi. They made it this far to find you. They aren't going to give up."

Elizabeth nodded.

"Okay you're right. Let's talk about something else. Why were you waiting for me today?"

She looked at him and for once his easy manner didn't come forward. His smile was on his face but not in his eyes.

"I came to check on you and the call. I just happened to go by Sweet Blooms and I sweetened the deal."

"Are you okay Henry?"

"I'm fine, let's get you some food. You must be hungry after last night."

Elizabeth nodded and went along with Henry, but all afternoon she felt the shadow of doubt following her around. Something was off and she didn't know what it was.

The night before Elizabeth had called Henry and told him that Smiley had made it out of surgery and he was cancer free. To celebrate they were going to go out on their first public date as an engaged couple. She thought about bringing Wi-Fi but decided they'd include her when they returned to the ranch.

They met at the park and she was surprised to see that Henry had gotten a Sweet Blooms basket for their lunch. He was dressed in a blue suit which gave her a moment pause, but she overcame that and walked into his arms.

"I see you're always prepared. Were you a boy scout?" she asked, pointing to the Sweet Blooms basket.

"I wish I could say I was but the truth of the matter is I don't like to be hungry. A growling stomach always ruins the mood."

Henry found an empty table by a tree. After he had spread out the goods on the table Elizabeth sat down and laughed.

"What's so funny?"

"You know Henry, this is one of the first times we've sat at a table to eat."

He looked around and then shrugged. "If you like this kind of thing I guess it's okay. Personally, I like to be near the pond."

"It's true, it's one of my favorite places as well."

Henry grinned. "You see we have a favorite place now. We are truly doing the couple thing."

"Okay you may have a point and be a great planner."

"Thank you, it's good for you to recognize my—"

Elizabeth held up her hand.

"Don't lose it. I can see your head is getting larger and larger already."

Henry laughed. "You make me laugh, Beth."

"You're just saying that because you think it will get you more of my food. It's not true. I'm not sharing my sweets."

He took a bite out of a sandwich and then wiggled his eyebrows.

"You say that now. Just wait until the sweets come out. I know all sorts of tricks, and dogs love me."

"Sure, they do. It's because you give them your sandwich as a bribe while you take the sweet stuff."

"Is this what the engagement banter is going to be about? Dogs and sweets?"

Elizabeth sniffed. "I think those are both great subjects. It shows you have good character if you have those interests."

"Ah, again your wisdom in all things floors me."

Elizabeth reached into the bag and pulled out a sweet. She opened her mouth and slowly closed on the sweet.

"MMmhh, this tart is amazing. I would share, but I'm not going to."

Both of them burst out laughing. It was the perfect day. Elizabeth felt happy and cared for. The sun was up and children ran around the park. She even saw a puppy or two frolicking on the grass. They were surrounded by people who didn't even notice them.

This was what she had been looking for. Someone to laugh with and someone she could trust. Then the reality of it settled on her. Henry was the person she had been looking for. He accepted her. He accepted the dogs. He was charming, funny and most of all she could trust him.

Before, she was worried about being seen in public, today she was confident. When he reached out and touched her hand she looked up and their eyes met. It would have been perfect if it hadn't been for that voice.

"Hello, Elizabeth."

Elizabeth wanted to ignore him and for Lance to just walk away. She knew that wasn't going to happen but while she was in the perfect-day fog she wanted to think on it a little while longer and hopefully it would come true.

When Lance cleared his throat and Henry looked at her with a small grin she knew she was going to have to talk to acknowledge him.

"Hello, Lance."

Henry looked at Lance and nodded. "Lance," he said. Elizabeth knew she was well and truly having feelings for Henry. She now thought his voice was amazing.

Lance looked at Henry. "You're still around?"

Then Lance turned to Elizabeth. "I bet you're feeling pretty smug with yourself right now."

Elizabeth shook her head. "Lance, I don't know what you're talking about. I have nothing to feel smug about."

"Sure, that's why you're out here in public, flaunting the fact that you're not paying me my due."

Lance switched to Henry. "Was it you? Did you tell her that she doesn't have to pay me?"

Henry never broke his gaze with Lance when he replied. "I didn't have to tell her anything. She already knew."

"She knew did she?" he sneered.

"She's a smart woman and yes, she knew all on her own."

For a moment Elizabeth thought that Lance would keep on, then she watched him take a step back and laugh.

Elizabeth had had enough. "Lance please go."

"Oh, oh, oh I get it now. You are playing my game? Yes, I can see it now."

Elizabeth was confused but as soon as Lance started to relax she could feel the self-doubt creep in. "Lance just go."

Lance stepped back and brushed his suit off.

"I'm going Elizabeth. You should have told me that you wanted to get taken by a country boy and I would have found a partner to help you out."

"What are you talking about?"

"I'm talking about your fiancée here, he's with you so that he can own your sanctuary. Didn't he tell you it's who owns the land that owns it all? He's not interested in you, why would he be?"

Elizabeth looked at Henry and waited for him to say something. She waited for him to say that Lance didn't know a thing. But the denial never came.

Then Henry did speak. "Lance you should go, you don't know Beth." He reached across the table and grabbed her hand. "She's a simple woman. She's beautiful inside and out. Her compassion is her guiding light and it helps to bring out the best in us all. She's the kind of woman that a man usually only has one chance to marry in a lifetime."

Elizabeth knew he was saying those things to make Lance go away. If only he would deny the big lie that Lance had said. If only he would say it wasn't true and that he wasn't the same as Lance. If only he'd say something to stop her heart from breaking.

"I never thought you'd settle Elizabeth, I guess I was wrong," he said. "If you're willing to throw it all away for him then best to you."

Elizabeth didn't see Lance walk away. She was numb sitting at the table. A few moments passed and the only thing she could think to do was to pack the basket.

"Beth?"

"I noticed you didn't deny it."

"Let me explain."

He needed to explain to her? She needed to go. Elizabeth stood up and walked out of the park. She didn't know anything except she needed to get to her car and she needed to be with Smiley.

She felt Henry touch her shoulder and then she jerked away from him. She held up her hand towards the blurry figure that was Henry.

"Don't, please don't touch me," she said in a low whisper.

"Beth—"

She shook her head. "There are no words for this. I need to think. Just let me think and I'll contact you later."

She didn't know how she made it to her car but when she got in it she couldn't move. She just laid her head on the wheel and cried.

<h1 style="text-align:center">Nineteen</h1>

It had ben two days since Beth had called him. He finally saw her today and she was carrying Wi-Fi to her crate. Work had already started on the crate house and by all accounts Beth should've been happy, but it was clear that she wasn't. What hurt the most was it was his fault.

For the last two days he'd seen Calla teaching the volunteers or Beth working with the construction crew. Today she was in the barn helping the volunteers do a general assessment of the dogs so they could classify which dogs needed to be isolated. He wanted to join the class. He was so desperate to hear her voice that it didn't even matter what she was saying.

After an hour of hands-on training the volunteers took their dogs back to their crates. Henry didn't even try to hide; he wanted to speak to her. When she was walking the volunteers to the front of the house, Elizabeth stopped in front of him.

"I'd like to speak to you when I come back?" she asked.

"Of course."

He waited until the last car had driven off. Then he saw Beth walking up the hill to him. If he didn't know any better he would think she was going to her execution. He could tell from her body language that this wasn't going to be a pleasant conversation. She walked into the barn and then she went to stand on the other side of the bench.

She lifted her head and he saw the dark circles under her eyes. When he was about to speak she held her hand out.

"Please let me speak. I want you to know that you've been really helpful to me," she began. "I came to you and I wasn't completely upfront with you and still you helped me out."

He nodded. "Anything for you Beth, you know that."

She didn't return the gesture. "After thinking on the whole issue I think I need to look for another place."

"You don't have to go."

She couldn't leave. She was everything to him. They had so much between them and now she was leaving? He could fix this if she would just give him the opportunity.

"I can't be angry with you when I wasn't upfront with you either. I want to say thank you for helping me and trying," she kept on.

"Beth don't walk away from us. Won't you give me a chance?"

"It's really better this way. I need to think and I'll let you know when I've got it setup. I'll pay you back for the construction. It might take me a minute but I'll get it to you."

"Beth, please fight for us," he demanded.

"Us? What us? I don't know that we ever really knew

each other at all. I don't want to play house anymore Henry. You might be okay with that but it's not for me."

He stood there and looked at her.

"Are you that scared that you'd say that to me?"

"I'm not scared. I'm realistic."

With those words she walked away and he stood there watching his dream walk away. He needed to let her go and find a way to get her back, if it was even possible.

Henry was cleaning out the stalls. It had been four days since Beth had left. He hadn't come up with an idea. He hadn't been able to really think at all. Her was at his wits end and was forced to consider that there wasn't a way to fix him and Beth.

He'd spent long nights just looking into the sky as if an answer would manifest. He'd gone over his life with a fine-toothed comb and he hadn't been able to find a reason for Beth to take him back either. He thought he had done so much. Henry thought that he had reformed but when it counted he was the same. He couldn't get himself together and it cost him dearly.

"Darn it, I hoped that Clarissa wasn't right but she was," Jerry said as he walked into the barn. "She said you'd be wallowing in your own hay and not moving a wit."

Henry looked up and saw Jerry in his blue jeans and white polo.

"Jerry?"

"Don't you be Jerrying me? Boy, do you know that I had to drive out here? You don't even have the decency to be depressed in town."

Henry shook his head and looked at Jerry and swallowed. "I messed up."

"I heard. It sounds like you forgot the number one rule."

Henry looked confused.

"The number one rule is if there is a secret, a woman will find it."

He shook his head. "I thought I could fix it before. I thought I could make it better but it just kept getting later and later until—"

"Until you got caught out there with no shorts and her ex went and painted you with the same brush as himself."

"What have I done, Jerry? She's everything and now she's gone."

Jerry put his hands over his ears. "Please stop! We knew you were slow. We know you did wrong. How long do you need to beat yourself up before you go and get the girl?"

Henry took a seat at the table and stared at Jerry. "And just how would you suggest I go ahead and do that?"

"The way every man has done it before you. Beg."

Elizabeth had been trying to get in contact with Mr. Zechy for a week. A week, that's how long ago it had been since she'd seen color. Every night had been a gamut of emotions that ran from despair that she had never known, to an anger that frightened her with its intensity. Out of the two she preferred the new emotion of anger. True it was scary, but she already knew where the feelings of depression led.

She had told herself she would never be a victim again. She'd never let herself down, but there were days like this when it felt like her hopes and dreams had been snatched from her. Still she got up every morning and refused to give in to the temptation of staying in bed and wallowing.

She hadn't heard from Henry and that was probably what hurt the most. It made no sense that after she told him it was over she still expected him to call her, but she did. Over the last week she realized how desperate and hard up she must have been. If what they had was based on desperation and pity it was best that it ended. Now she just needed to convince herself of that.

Elizabeth walked into the hotel lobby and Clarissa was standing in the middle of it looking around. Elizabeth almost didn't recognize her because she was in blue jeans, sneakers, a white t-shirt and her hair was in a sloppy pony tail. When she spotted Elizabeth she made a beeline for her.

"Clarissa?"

"Please, just please. I knew you would be wallowing. I tell you I know people when it comes to self-sabotaging. Anyway I've got to go, Bain and I are going away for a couple of days. I wanted to do something for you, so I had them move your bags and belongings to the suite. It's the best room in the hotel. While that might not be saying a whole lot it will be comfier than where you were."

"Really Clarissa, I appreciate it but—"

Clarissa leaned down and kissed her on the cheek. "No time to hear your protests just so you can do what I want you to do anyway. Enjoy your room and remember you only have one life, hold on to it. Bain is waiting, I've got to go."

Elizabeth watched Clarissa practically skip out to meet Bain. Clarissa was going to meet the man of her dreams. She went to the elevator feeling lost and alone. Now she would be in an even larger room to remind her of the fact she was alone. When she got to the floor there was only one door. That door was ajar. Just what she needed a maid still cleaning up.

The aroma that floated out of the room was one of flowers and warm sugar. Curiosity brought her closer and when she opened the door, inside were candles everywhere. The floor was covered in red rose petals and there was a statue of a butler by the door holding a plate with a note.

Please remove your shoes, it said.

She stepped in and closed the door. She took off her shoes and the feel of petals beneath her feet at first tickled. She gave a little laugh before she could stop it. On the back of the door were post it notes with messages like:

Beth is beautiful.
Beth is loving.
Beth is worthy.
Beth is amazing.

As she read the notes she had to hold back the tears that threatened to fall. Blinking the tears away she turned to the petal path. She took two steps and then she heard Henry's voice saying,

"I'm sorry Beth."

She stepped back because she didn't see him but when she stepped forward it happened again. She looked at the ground and every time her foot passed the light it spoke. She continued down the path and every two feet she heard Henry's voice saying.

"You're my light Beth."

"Without you the pond is just a pond."

"Without you I'm just existing."

She was half way through the living room when she saw the bedroom door cracked. When she pushed into the room there was a table set for dinner and on the other side of it dressed in a dark suit was Henry.

She knew she missed him but seeing him now, just how much she missed him hit her. He wasn't her fake engagement, he was her friend. If she were honest she would have to say that a friend making a mistake isn't a reason to break up. The problem wasn't Henry and the truth. The problem was her and her fear to trust.

Henry stepped around the table and held out his hand.

"Beth, trust me. I'll do better, but I need you."

This was the moment. She stood there looking at his hand. All of him looked good. In that dark suit he looked like he was ready to sweep her away. The way the suit fitted his chest and the way his jaw was set as if he was ready for the fight.

"I think we've hurt each other long enough," he said.

"Henry?"

"I made a mistake. It won't be the last one but no matter what, we need to talk about our issues."

Elizabeth looked at him, confident and strong. She had to tell him she was really a coward. She looked up, ready to tell him and then he reached out and pulled her into his arms.

"Don't doubt us. We are stronger together than anything. Will you take a chance with me?"

A few minutes ago, she would have never thought

this was possible, now she was going to take Clarissa's advice and live life to the fullest.

She reached up and wrapped her arms around his neck. "You couldn't get rid of me if you tried."

The moment his lips touched hers she knew she had made the right decision and she had found a man who was strong, and made her laugh. Her future looked brighter than ever before.

I hope you enjoyed Elizabeth and Henry's story.

If you enjoyed this series, you could check out some of my other series:

Love Endures series. Clean and Wholesome love doesn't just happen in small towns, they can happen in cities too. Second chance love stories that prove that love endures.

Silver Fox series. Love comes to us in all stages of life. Celebrate the couples that find life after kids have grown up and sometimes even after our first loves have passed.

Love Saves series. Sweet romantic comedy where couples find out what really matters in their lives, how opposites can do more than just attract and how love can save us all.

Sign up for my newsletter to receive updates on new releases and promotions.

susanwarnerauthor.com

www.ingramcontent.com/pod-product-compliance
Lightning Source LLC
Chambersburg PA
CBHW071821190726
48292CB00005B/1542